6/10

Hiroshima Dreams

Also by

Kelly Easton

Hiroshima Dreams

Kelly Easton

DUTTON CHILDREN'S BOOKS

DUTTON CHILDREN'S BOOKS
A division of Penguin Young Readers Group

Published by the Penguin Group
Penguin Group (USA) Inc., 375 Hudson Street, New York, New York 10014, U.S.A.
Penguin Group (Canada), 90 Eglinton Avenue East, Suite 700, Toronto, Ontario, Canada
M4P 2Y3 (a division of Pearson Penguin Canada Inc.) • Penguin Books Ltd, 80 Strand,
London WC2R 0RL, England • Penguin Ireland, 25 St Stephen's Green, Dublin 2, Ireland
(a division of Penguin Books Ltd) • Penguin Group (Australia), 250 Camberwell Road,
Camberwell, Victoria 3124, Australia (a division of Pearson Australia Group
Pty Ltd) • Penguin Books India Pvt Ltd, 11 Community Centre, Panchsheel Park,
New Delhi - 110 017, India • Penguin Group (NZ), 67 Apollo Drive, Rosedale,
North Shore 0745, Auckland, New Zealand (a division of Pearson New Zealand Ltd)
Penguin Books (South Africa) (Pty) Ltd, 24 Sturdee Avenue, Rosebank,
Johannesburg 2196, South Africa • Penguin Books Ltd, Registered Offices:
80 Strand, London WC2R 0RL, England

This book is a work of fiction. Names, characters, places, and incidents
are either the product of the author's imagination or are used fictitiously,
and any resemblance to actual persons, living or dead,
business establishments, events, or locales is entirely coincidental.

The publisher does not have any control over and does not assume any responsibility
for author or third-party websites or their content.

CIP Data is available.

Published in the United States by Dutton Children's Books,
a division of Penguin Young Readers Group
345 Hudson Street, New York, New York 10014
www.penguin.com/youngreaders

Designed by Elizabeth Frances

Printed in USA   First Edition
ISBN 978-0-525-47821-8   10 9 8 7 6 5 4 3 2 1

For my husband, Michael Ruben,
and our children: Isaac, Isabelle, Mollie, and Rebecca.

Many thanks to my lovely editor, Maureen Sullivan, who understood the voice and spirit of this book. Thanks to Michele Coppola, who asked me to write a book about "someone with special gifts," and to all the others at Dutton Children's Books who have worked so hard on Hiroshima Dreams.

Thank you to my persistent and good-humored agent, Michael Bourret of Dystel and Goderich, to Herb Ruben for offering me research materials, to Charlotte Ruben for proofreading, to Jean Brown, and to my readers: Marilynn Easton and Randall Easton Wickham.

Each and every heart it seems
is bounded by a world of dreams.
—Moody Blues, "The Voice"

Hiroshima Dreams

Lotus Seeds

I have the gift of vision. It was given to me by my grandma, handed to me in a lotus seed, a pod that felt as big as my five-year-old hand.

That was when she came to us from Japan, bowing repeatedly to my father, an American, to show him respect, to tell him how grateful she was that she would not be alone.

My sister, Sally, then eight, skipped circles around Grandma, flipped her Prom Barbie high in the air, and caught it with one hand. Sally informed Grandma that we were stopping at McDonald's on the way home, which wasn't true. Our mother had made udon and fish cakes, yakisoba, dragon roll, sashimi, tamago, tuna in ponzu sauce, and tempura. Our dad was ecstatic; he loved Japanese food, but Mom usually refused to make it. She had a Betty Crocker cookbook, which couldn't be pried away from her. She'd won the local Betty Crocker contest three times.

The waiting area of the airport was full of rushing people. I wondered what it would feel like to be so important that you had to move fast.

I stood in the terminal in my winter coat and gloves and watched everything. It is what I do, the world entering me through my eyes, my body incidental. The world. My eyes. That's it.

"Yes," Grandma said in perfect English, crossing over to me, planting the smooth seed in my palm. "You are the one."

MU

Spring, 1996

Koans and Cones

On the drive home from the airport, Grandma speaks to Mom in Japanese. Her voice reminds me of an instrument; not one I have ever played, like the cello, but a rare one from another time and place.

Mom's replies come out stiffly. It is as if her words are tin men waiting to be oiled. I've never heard her speak Japanese.

Grandma turns and hands small bags to Sally and to me: "Tea candies. You try. The wrapper will melt in your mouth."

"Thank you," Sally says, then she elbows me because I am silent.

I untie the twine from the plastic bag and slide the pale

green candy into my mouth. At first I can't taste anything, only the wrapper dissolving against my tongue.

"Do you know what a koan is?" Grandma asks us.

"An ice cream!" Sally volunteers. "My favorite is mint chocolate chip. The Creamery has twenty-five flavors. Maybe more. They have an Awful Awful, which is the thickest milk shake you can imagine. Can we stop there, Mom?"

"No!"

"This kind of koan is a story," Grandma explains. "Not ice cream. A puzzle to bring you closer to God."

"You mean Jesus?" Sally's voice is suspicious. She hates church and catechism, despises the nuns, who she says look like black crows ready to swoop down and peck out your eyes.

"*You* know," Dad insists. "Like, 'What is the sound of one hand clapping,' or, 'If a tree falls in the forest and no one is there to hear it, does it still make a sound?'"

Grandma narrows her eyes, like she suddenly remembers that it was he who stole Mom away from Japan.

The delicate green tea flavor expands in my mouth like a dusk made of honey.

"Tell us one," Sally demands.

Grandma closes her eyes, then opens them. "A monk asked his students, 'Will the petals of the flowers return to the trees?' The students rustled and shoved, each one hoping to be first with the right answer. The first answered: 'The petals will renew themselves when spring comes.' The second said: 'When the wind comes they will be blown back up into the branches.' The third shouted: 'Some trees do not flower at all. It depends upon the trees.' But the monk shook his head. 'Come back in a few years,' he told them all, 'when you are ready for enlightenment.'"

Sally holds up her Barbie to the window to watch the gray streaks of sky above the freeway. Then she grabs a pen off the floor and makes elaborate designs on her leg, where Mom won't see; Sally will doodle on *anything*.

A thought flies into my mind, lands with the lightness of a butterfly, but I know it is wrong. Still, I volunteer. "The monk's students answered too quickly. And they cared too much about winning."

Mom and Dad laugh. Sally says, "It speaks. What do you know? I thought its tongue was frozen to its mouth."

"Don't call your sister *it*," Mom scolds.

Not to be upstaged, Sally says, "Remember those monks in Maine who sing and make jam? They wore long dresses like girls."

"Different kind of monk," Dad says.

"I knew I was right about you," Grandma whispers to me.

After that, Grandma says nothing for a while. Like Barbie, she watches out the window of the car. Her shoulders droop. Something droops inside of me, too, like after a boy in my kindergarten poured yellow paint on my sunflower plant to "make it look like it was supposed to."

Although it is April, there is snow on the ground. The

plows have shoved it into banks that look like dirty Styrofoam. We pass the giant blue insect on top of the pest company and a billboard for Building 19 that says, DON'T COMPLAIN ABOUT OUR FREE COFFEE. SOMEDAY YOU'LL BE WEAK AND OLD, TOO. Another billboard shows a magical castle. It says DISNEY WORLD.

"Hirohito," Grandma mutters.

"What?" Mom says.

"The emperor. That skunk."

"Why did you think about that?" Mom asks.

"*He* went to that Disney place. Disneyland. Strolled down the street with Mickey Mouse, as if he hadn't started a war at all."

"That emperor is history," Mom says. "The new one, though; he seems nice. His wife hasn't produced an heir."

"That's the prince," Grandma corrects. "He won't be emperor until his father dies. Remember, his father was the first emperor to marry a commoner."

It sounds so amazing to me: an emperor, a prince, like Japan is one of the fairy tales Mom used to read me before I could read to myself.

"We live in the historic area." Dad veers onto the exit ramp. "Speaking of history."

We drive past the factory with broken windows, the mall, the train station, and the university, into our neighborhood. I love the giant trees lining the sidewalk, the old houses painted in the dark colors of fall.

"This is all yours?" Grandma says as we pull into the driveway.

"The house is divided into two apartments," Dad explains. "But once, it was a whole house."

"Oh."

"It's a three-bedroom," Mom says. "Our part is sixteen hundred square feet."

"That's big."

"By Japanese standards." Mom shrugs.

"It was built in 1860," Dad says.

"In 1860? Historic? Ah. This is a young country."

The stairs are icy, so Dad holds Grandma's elbow as she walks up.

"It is spring and yet it is so cold here." She shivers. "Ishiguro Yoko moved to America with *her* daughter and she says the sun always shines. She wears T-shirts every day. I thought I might call on her."

"Yoko lives in California, Mom. This is New England. You would have to get on a plane to call on her." My mom's voice sounds pinched, like it does before she has friends over and everything has to be just right.

"But you can certainly *call* her on the phone," Dad offers. He always wants everyone to be happy.

"*Mom?*" Grandma mimics, ignoring Dad's offer.

"This is America," Mom replies.

"But you are called *Mom*. I must be Sobo or . . . Obaachan. Yes, I think, Obaachan."

"Obaachan." Dad opens the door and motions us in. Mom rushes to the kitchen and pulls the covers off the food she's spent the whole day preparing. "You must be hungry."

Obaachan peers at the apartment: the painting of cowboys and Indians, the TV, the old gray couch, and the kitchen counter lined with food. I can see from her face how her stomach feels. It feels the way mine did when I walked into kindergarten that first day, and it seemed like every kid was staring at me.

"Yes," she lies. "Hungry."

During dinner, Mom chatters away about all of the things Obaachan will love about America: the malls, the freeways, the ocean, the eighty channels on the TV, *The Oprah Winfrey Show*, and the Food Network. Sally glares at her plate and shoves the food around. Her idea of a meal is something that comes in a bag, a burger, chicken fingers, french fries, a shake, at the very least meat loaf or fried chicken.

Obaachan holds up the fork. "It gives food a tin taste. Yes?"

"You can get more in your mouth at once," Mom argues.

"We have chopsticks." Dad gets up and searches through a drawer. He picks out one wooden stick and one black one, but doesn't find a match. "At least we used to."

"This is fine." Obasaan lifts a forkful of rice to her mouth. "I will get more in my mouth. Very good food, Shoujo. Thank you."

"Are you still in touch with Shizuko Yamamoto?" Mom asks.

"Oh, yes. Always. We had a business together before I left. It was doing well. She cried so much at the airport, I thought she would make a flood."

"Do you want to give her a call and tell her you arrived safely?" Dad says. Mom gives him a look. She doesn't like long-distance phone calls.

"It is not necessary. She will know. Thank you."

My room has been given to Obaachan, so I am now with Sally. At bedtime, Sally takes a string and makes a line across the room. "Don't cross that line unless I say so. I get the bigger side because I'm older and this is *my* room. Don't touch my things. Don't whine in your sleep." She throws her tea candies to my side. "Those are gross."

I take the tea candies and hide them under my pillow in case she changes her mind and wants them back.

I go out to kiss my mom and dad good night. My dad picks me up and tosses me in the air. "Sack of potatoes." He pretends to gobble me up.

"You're too rough with her," Mom says. "She's small."

"Light as a feather." He tosses me again.

Mom frowns. "Did you eat enough, Lin?"

"She ate more than anyone, for once," Dad says. "She likes Japanese food, too."

"It gave me indigestion," Mom says.

I help Dad carry an electric heater into Obaachan's room. He brings her extra blankets.

"Have my boxes come yet?" Obaachan asks.

"No," Dad assures her, "but I'm sure they will soon."

"I mailed them weeks ago."

"They'll come. So glad you are here."

"Good night . . . Grandma Obaachan," I say.

"Good night, Lin. Good night, Bobby-San. Imagine, we used to be enemies." She bows to us and closes the door.

"What did she mean by that?" I ask Dad. "'We used to be enemies.'"

"She was talking about a war. It happened a long time ago."

"How long?"

"Over fifty years ago."

"What was it about?"

"War is never about anything but greed. But don't worry, Lin. It was far in the past. People are wiser now."

Being an Ant

There is a word used about me, whispered like a secret. It is said by my mom at cooking exhibitions when I hide behind the food table, by my sister to her friends, by my teacher to my dad when he drops me off at school. The word reminds me of the empty bird's nest in our oak tree, or the cactus on the windowsill in our kitchen, hidden among the ladles and pot holders.

SHY

I am most shy at school, where the squirming bodies of the other kids make me feel like an ant in a room of giants.

In the morning we have free play, which is not too bad. I do puzzles, read books, and watch the giants. Cora Wilson has big eyes and long blond hair. She reminds me of one of the ladies at the Miss America pageant. She could have a crown put on her head and walk down the long ramp, and it would never fall off.

Sam Kline and Charlie Mills pretend to play with LEGOs, but when the teacher isn't looking, they fight. Ahab, Walter, and Irma, who looks and acts like a boy, pretend to be Pokémon trainers. Irma seems to have fun, but I get a funny feeling when I look at her, like something is wrong. Once, her dad came to pick her up early. He was smoking a cigarette. When the teacher told him to put it out, he dropped it right on the floor and smashed it with his foot.

Matt Perino sits on the rug with a book, looking at the pictures, like my dad studying a map when we're lost and he doesn't want to ask for directions. Matt is sometimes alone, sometimes with others. He does what he wants.

Something about Matt makes me feel different, like we're friends even though we don't play together. Maybe he's special because his dad is a policeman. On some days, he's dropped off at school in a black-and-white police car. When he hops out of that car, it's like he's some king. Everyone watches.

Circle time is the worst. We sit on the alphabet carpet and answer questions from the teacher, like: "What do you imagine when you look at the sky?" Or, "If you were a hat, what kind would you be?"

Each child is supposed to take a turn. I always have many ideas and answers: if I were a hat, I'd be a feather hat, or a snake coiled round, or maybe the hat from *Go Dog Go*, dripping with dog bones, confetti, and party favors, the one the boy dog finally likes. But when it's my turn, and all eyes are on me, my voice is an elevator stuck between floors. If I am lucky, I might be able to whisper. Usually, though, I am as silent as Obaachan's room.

The day after she came, I waited for her to come out, and to tell me why I was "the one." But the door never opened. Mom told me to be patient and to let Grandma rest. That was a week ago.

"We'll come back to you later, Lin." The teacher smiles. I study the letters on the carpet, each square fitting together like a puzzle. And she never comes back to me later. I have a feeling she was once like me and understands.

Nap time is the one time of the day I love. We lie out on towels like sunbathers on the beach. The child who is stillest wins a lollipop. I win it many times, until Cora complains: "But Teacher, she's like that even when she's not on the towel."

Irma says, "Lin is a statue."

After that, I win less often, even though I am still. If I am already a statue, I guess it is less of an accomplishment.

After nap time, there's show-and-tell. Walter always brings in a sports thing, like a signed baseball, or a card he's gotten out of gum. Cora brings black patent leather shoes with bows that snap on, and a talking doll. Matt brings in his dad's police badge. I want to bring in Obaachan, to tug her out of her room, and let her speak for me. She could wear the kimono she arrived in and tell a magic koan to the class, like she did in the car. "Don't be ridiculous, Lin," Mom says when I ask her. "She won't leave her room, let alone the house. She is so shy of this country."

"Were you shy, when you first got here?"

Mom doesn't answer. "You can bring your Wet Cathy doll for show-and-tell." Mom has given me a doll that goes pee. The doll has blond curly hair, and big blue eyes that close when you lay her down. That doll gives me nightmares. I dream she comes to life and chases me. I dream she pees so much she makes a flood that rises as high as the ceiling.

After Mom kisses me good night and leaves the room, I hide the doll. Wet Cathy is one of those things that Mom expects of me. I should have fun at kindergarten and make friends. I should be more like Sally. I should love the doll. But she looks nothing like me.

Even so, if she were a talking doll, with a string that pulled words from her mouth, like the one Cora has, then maybe . . . maybe I would bring her.

A Closed Door

The door to Obaachan's room remains closed for two weeks, although there are signs of her: the rustling of paper and the sound of boxes (which finally arrive), the scent of jasmine, gardenia oil, incense, and green tea.

From outside the door, I try to remind Obaachan that we are here, waiting. During my cello lesson, I play as loudly as possible so she'll hear. Ms. Nga, my teacher, scolds me: "Volume is not the result we're looking for, Lin. It is subtlety."

Sally rushes in to offer her opinion of my music. "Did a cat die? I heard someone murdering a cat." Sally once had her own lessons, at piano. Her teacher was a man named Gustav. He taped thumbtacks on the keys he didn't want her to strike so that she would get poked if she made a mistake. "Meeeowww," Sally howls. "I'm dying."

She does sound like a dying cat.

Ms. Nga takes a swipe at Sally with her bow. Sally jumps back and runs out of the room. "Now, Lin," Ms. Nga instructs. "Think of the notes as being round and sweet, like little chocolates that float in the sky. You are speaking *sweetly* for the composer." I try to imagine candy in the air. My mouth waters as I play.

Still Obaachan's door doesn't open. In contrast to the other sounds of our house—the voices, the loud Barbie sagas that Sally enacts with her friend Molly, the television, Mom's kitchen utensils and phone conversations, and the rustle of Dad's newspaper, Obaachan's room is an island of quiet. I have a name for the room. I call it *Mystery*. The silence of that mystery is louder than any noise.

That weekend, the temperature soars. The snow melts to a muddy slush. Buds appear like fists on the trees waiting to open their fingers into petals.

This year, Sally's birthday and Easter are on the same day. The priest has spent the morning hiding plastic eggs in the church. After mass, he rings a bell and the children dash through the reception room.

If it wasn't for Sally I would get nothing; the other children are so much faster and more forceful than I am. But Sally beats them all; she gets the most filled eggs, then she scatters half of her winnings in the church for only me to find.

At our house, we live at the kitchen table. On it, when we come home, is an Easter bunny cake that Mom has made. The bunny cake stands straight up on its hind legs and is covered in pink and yellow frosting. Sally cries when Mom goes to cut it, so we don't eat the bunny. Instead it's placed on top of the fridge, a triumph of baking powder over gravity.

Although Obaachan still doesn't come out, she leaves a present for Sally wrapped in rice paper. It is a tiny straw doll in a red-and-white kimono. Inside its hand is a little scroll with words in Japanese. "What does it say?" Sally asks Mom.

Mom squints at the characters. "Many blessings."

Sally slides the doll across the table to me. "You can have it."

"It's raining." Mom points out the window.

"I wish my birthday was July Fourth, like Lin's," Sally says. "It's always warm and sunny."

"April in New England is nothing but another March," Dad complains. In our house, *he* is the foreigner with his red hair and freckles. There is no sign on us that he is our dad.

April reminds me of Sally, actually, sulky and teasing much of the time, then once in a while letting out a smile.

Mom puts candles in mint chocolate chip ice cream. Sally blows out all nine of them in one breath, then says her wish out loud. "I want my room back to myself."

"Shhh, Sally." Dad looks toward the mysterious door.

"Wishes don't come true if you say them out loud," I gripe, because I like being in Sally's room, even in my roped-off half.

"Get a life." Sally folds her arms.

"She's your grandmother, our family," Mom whispers.

"Molly's grandma takes her shopping at Providence Place. She buys her a new wardrobe every time the weather even hints at a change. She takes her to Fire and Ice to eat."

"You always talk about Molly," I nag.

"Obaachan doesn't even *try* to join our family, or to be American."

"When you get to a certain age," Dad explains, "it's hard to change."

"Well, she should get a life."

"Everyone should get a life, according to you," Mom says.

The door creaks open, then. Obaachan appears in sweatpants and a black turtleneck, her long gray hair piled on top of her head. Her skin looks like the rice paper.

Dad, Mom, and Sally stare at her, as if she were a ghost, but I peer past her into my old bedroom. The high shelves that held my trinkets and books now contain strange objects: stones, statues, vases, photographs, and woodcuts. A sweet scent escapes, curls around us like smoke, reminding me of mornings when we go to church and Mom kneels at the pew mumbling Hail Marys and Our Fathers.

"I was a little tired from my trip," Obaachan explains.

Sally's face goes bright red. She grabs the doll back from me.

"So . . ." Mom's voice is singsong and false. "What were you doing? Sleeping?"

"Meditating."

"Meditating." Mom taps her foot. I know that tap. I saw it when the lamp was broken and Sally said the wind blew it over, when Dad lost his fifth lunch pail in a month, and when Sally's teacher sent home a note about her talking in class. "About what?"

"*Mu.*"

"Like the cow?" Sally says.

Obaachan peers at my mom. "You remember?"

"No. I don't remember much about the past." Mom says it like an accusation. "I tend to focus on the future."

"The present is also nice," Obaachan says.

"We're having mint ice cream." I grab a bowl and scoop ice cream into it. Dad pulls another chair to the table.

"Sally's favorite." Obaachan sits down and tastes the ice cream. "I am ready to be American."

One Hand Clapping

Kindergarten ends in June. It is a relief except when I remember that next year, I will go to the big school, where there are even more giants stomping through the huge building.

Sally's friend Molly is discarded after she breaks the head off Sally's Beach Barbie in a fit of anger, and is replaced by a girl named Marigold Strauss, who lives across the street.

Marigold has a round freckled face, brown hair that reaches past her waist, and an orange cat she carries everywhere, also called Marigold. Aside from that, the most noticeable thing about her is how often she talks about God: "God, could you believe Helen Frankel's barrettes. They looked like dead cockroaches. Oh-my-God! When Jimmy Baker let out that fart in the swimming pool, I almost puked. God, is that embarrassing or what? For God's sake, at least he could go to the bathroom. God, I want to be one of the Spice Girls in the worst way."

Marigold's house is not sectioned into pieces. They live in the entire thing. Her father is a professor at Brown University. Her mother paints portraits of celebrities and other important people. Her name is Daisy, after someone in a book called *The Great Gatsby*, she tells Mom. Daisy lets Sally come over each day while our parents are at work. "God, I get so much done when Sally comes over," Daisy tells Mom.

"Maybe we should change Sally's name to Rose; then they could have a whole flowerpot over there," Dad says, joking.

Since I'm not invited, Mom brings me to work with her at Lutz Cutz. Many heads pass through my mom's hands each day. Many voices scatter their stories and secrets, like the tufts of hair dropping to the floor.

Or she puts strips of foil on the women's heads so that they look like space aliens, then they sit under helmets of hot air, like astronauts; the salon as spaceship, my mom the captain.

I sit in whatever swivel chair is empty and study my face in the mirror. I try to imagine my future, which seems as distant as Saturn. I can picture myself in a smock like my mother's, only mine is white and I am not standing in one place, I am moving.

The women talk and talk. Sometimes I know what they are

going to say before they say it. "My daughter gave birth." "I was at a funeral." "I have a new job." "I won a tennis match." The words come into my head like they are my own, natural as tasting your own tongue. It makes me wonder about time, whether maybe we live it at different speeds. Like they have said it and I've heard it, because my time is quicker, and their time is slower. It's the only way I can explain the knowing I so often have, what people will say or do, what might happen.

Often, Mom makes the women's hair look like Wet Cathy's. My mom's own black hair is cut short, almost like a boy's. The long hair in her wedding photo is kept in a hatbox at the back of her closet. Sally showed it to me once, and two silk kimonos like Obaachan's: one bright red with gold leaves; the other, blue with purple fans. I never understood why Mom would choose gray pants and a black sweater over that beautiful fabric, or short hair instead of a long, thick mane.

There are three other ladies who work with Mom: Betty, Clarabel, and Simone. When there is a lull in business, Simone plays cards with me. We play Crazy Eights, Go Fish, and Old Maid. Clarabel brings me coloring books.

The salon is one of five owned by Bernard Lutz. On Tuesdays, Mr. Lutz comes in and sits at a table "doing the books." Just before he arrives, the ladies dump out their coffees and spit out their gum. They throw their snacks away. Betty and Clarabel put out their cigarettes and spray the room with air freshener. Then they all stand straight and focus on the heads in front of them like they are serious artists sculpting clay.

Just before Mr. Lutz gets there, Mom walks me to the bakery, and Mary, who owns it, watches me. She pounds bread dough with her fists and tells me about her husband, Hans, who came from Germany when he was seventeen and helped his father run the bakery. She complains how Hans tasted his pastries so much and so often that one day, he couldn't fit in the door and had to retire. Now Mary runs it by herself. Sometimes, I get to frost the cupcakes with her, then eat one.

Three weeks of summer pass this way. Then, one morning, on a Friday, Mr. Lutz walks in. He's the first man I've ever seen who wears jewelry: gold chains around his neck, rings on every finger, even his pinky.

There's no time to dump coffees or put out cigarettes, or to rush me to Mary's bakery. Everyone just goes completely still like they're playing freeze tag.

"I heard this little one is a real fixture here, Marge." Mr. Lutz points at me.

"It's fun for her to come to work sometimes," Mom says.

Lutz makes a face. "Harsh chemicals. No good for a child. And customers worry. Why is some kid just sitting here, hour after hour, day after day, doing nothing?"

"The ladies seem to really enjoy her. She cheers the place up."

"This isn't a day-care center."

"No. I know." Mom stares at the floor. Her cheeks flush. She sweeps a few clumps of hair aside with her foot. I am embarrassed to be the cause of such trouble.

"We need to put Lin in a summer program," Mom tells Dad at dinner. "Even at half-day, it's eighty dollars a week. And then I'll have to cut my hours."

Mom has made a pot roast, mashed potatoes and gravy, green beans, Caesar salad, and a blueberry pie. When my mom makes American food, Obaachan eats very little.

"Why can't she go to Marigold's house with Sally?" Dad asks.

"No way!" Sally snaps. "We have activities planned for every day. They don't include babysitting."

"I'm afraid that might be imposing too much on Mrs. Strauss," Mom says. "Already, she's watching Sally for free."

"You mean, I'm watching *Marigold*. It takes all my energy to keep that girl out of trouble."

"What?" Mom and Dad say together.

"Just joking." Sally gives a fake smile.

"What kind of trouble?" Mom says.

"Nothing. I'm just not bringing the baby with us."

"Where is the summer program?" Dad asks.

"At the Y."

"Don't put her there!" Sally says. "That place is swarming with kids, and there's barely any supervision. She'll fall into the swimming pool, and she won't even be able to open her mouth and call for help. She'll drown and no one will notice."

"Don't be so dramatic, Sally," Dad says.

"She'll be miserable."

"Eighty dollars a week." Dad shakes his head.

"*I* will take care of Lin," Obaachan says.

"You?" Mom says. "But you don't feel well."

"Well, she's hardly a wild monkey swinging in the trees. It will be easy."

"Really, we couldn't impose on you," Dad says.

"I am not working and I am perfectly capable of taking care of Lin."

"Well . . ."

"Okay with you, kiddo?" Dad asks.

I remember Dad saying the koan about the sound of one hand clapping.

This is it. Her presence. Her offer.

One hand. Invisible. And definitely clapping.

Spiderwebs

The next morning, when Obaachan comes to breakfast, Mom offers her green tea. "I'll take coffee," Obaachan says. "It smells very good. Like burned incense at the Year of the Tiger Festival."

Dad gets up and pours her a mug.

"See. I am becoming American."

Sally slumps in and sits at the table. "Someone took a bite out of this doughnut already."

"That's because it's *my* doughnut, Sally," Dad says, "on my plate, right where I was sitting. The box is on the counter."

"Get a life, Dad."

"Get a doughnut, Sally."

"Sleep well?" Mom asks Obaachan.

"I've lost my ability to dream."

"You don't dream?" Sally asks.

"I always dream the same dream. That's the problem. Smoke and flames."

"Sounds like a nightmare," Dad says.

"It was." Obaachan grimaces at her first sip of coffee. "So many Japanese are now drinking coffee. The letter from Shizuko says they are opening a Starbucks next year in the Ginza District."

Dad tugs his plate from Sally. "Now pass me the paper."

"He reads the news three times over," Mom says. "There's the *Providence Journal*, the *New York Times*, and the *Boston Globe*. He's the best informed person in the country."

"If you know history," Obaachan says, "you don't need the newspaper. It always repeats itself."

"I don't think that's true," Mom argues. "Why, think about technology. It changes the world. And President Clinton is bringing peace everywhere, even in Ireland."

"Listen to this," Dad says. "There's a pancake in Alabama that has the face of Mother Mary on it. It's been on display at the restaurant for three years without getting mold."

The phone rings. "It's Nora," I say.

"Hello." Mom answers. "Nora. Oh, wonderful. Yes. Just bring rose water and nasturtiums. They're edible. And the seashell molds. I'm on my way."

"It's creepy how you do that," Sally says.

"What?" I ask.

"Know who it is when the phone rings."

"It's always Nora."

"No, it's not. A lot of time it's for me. Even Dad gets an occasional call."

"Even *Dad*?" he says.

"I have to go. Nora was supposed to set up for the dessert competition, but she's running late, so I have to do it."

"Uh-huh," Dad says.

"The world is coming to an end," Mom says louder.

"Uh-huh."

Mom musses Dad's hair. "You're in charge, now. Get Sally to Marigold's. Sally, clean your side of the room when you get home."

"Bring home some leftovers," Sally says.

"Bye." Mom looks nervously at Obaachan. "You're sure Lin is not too much for you?"

"We'll be fine."

"You done, Sally?" Dad sets the paper down. "Come on. I'll walk you over to Marigold's on my way out."

"I'm not a baby."

"Then I don't have to change your diaper? What a relief. Come on, kiddo."

"Just stand at the corner. Don't walk me to the door. I'm not—"

"—a baby. I know."

"Ah, silence," Obaachan says when the house is finally ours. "It's a most beautiful sound."

Is it a sound? I wonder.

"Truth hides in silence, as you well know."

Do I?

"Now, what would you like to do? Play a game?"

I would like to go in her room and learn the stories of the statues and candles, the silk cloth, wooden shoes, and kimonos. I would like to see the objects that came out of the many boxes that arrived at our doorstep from a brown truck. But Mom has told me that she would invite me in if she wanted.

"Let's go in the backyard," I suggest.

"Yes." Obaachan nods. "I should do that. I've hardly stepped outside since I arrived."

We share a yard with our downstairs neighbor, Mr. Caros, a Portuguese man who yells at his wife. Once, when she was hanging laundry up, he came outside and yanked the clean clothes to the ground and stomped on them.

It's a small yard surrounded by different trees—pine, birch, blue spruce, and maple—as if the person who planted them couldn't make up their mind. There is a plot of grass, a brick patio, two Adirondack chairs, and a table. The chairs belong to

Mr. Caros, but he lets us use them; he saves his meanness for his wife.

I bring out Checkers and Go Fish. We play until lunch. Obaachan makes fried fish and rice with cabbage and pickled cucumbers for lunch. Then she naps under the trees while I practice my cello and paint watercolors. I keep thinking how lucky I am to have an obaachan, and not to be in camp with a bunch of other kids bumping and yelling, forced to speak up and act like the others.

After lunch, I bring out my favorite book, *Curious George*. "This is George. He lives in Africa . . ." I read to Obaachan about George trying on the man's yellow hat and being captured, phoning the fire department, and flying away with balloons. Then I read her another where George rides a bike. He's supposed to deliver newspapers, but he makes them into boats.

"You know who George reminds me of?" Obaachan says.

"Sally." That is why I love the book.

"Exactly. Aren't you young to be able to read?"

"The only other person in my kindergarten who could read was Matt Perino," I say, "and he's already six." Then I turn my face away so she won't see me blush; it is very bad to brag.

"Do you see that spiderweb?" She points. "When the spider casts its web, the first thread is tossed into the wind. Wherever the wind blows, the web will be built. It is the insect version of destiny."

"What is destiny?"

"It is the story the universe has written for us."

"Do we always have to obey the story?"

"You can try not to. But things work out better for us if we do."

"How do you know the story?"

"You feel it." She pats her stomach. "Here."

"Tell me a riddle, please. A koan like before, and I'll answer it."

When Obaachan smiles, the crinkles around her eyes draw all the way down her face. "You don't *have* to answer a koan. It is something to meditate upon. But I'll try to find one you can answer. Let's see. 'What is the difference between watching the whole world and watching one spider?'"

Remembering about the students who answered too fast, I take my time. I watch the spider sleep in its perfect web. "There is no difference."

"Yes, I think that's right. Each is equally sacred. Everything in life is sacred. It is only man who puts himself above other creatures, who is removed from the soul of animals, insects, plants, and trees."

"Girls," Mr. Caros booms from his doorway. "Food and entertainment." He carries a tray with lemonade and cookies and sings "Nessun dorma" and "O Sole Mio."

Obaachan claps her hands. "You sing so beautifully, and my granddaughter loves cookies."

"Italian opera," he says. "In my soul, I am Italian. And to see you two lovely ladies enjoying this beautiful day moved my heart to sing. Now . . . back to work."

After he is gone, Obaachan stares at the space where he stood. She is completely still, like she is looking at a painting on the wall of a museum. "He is a big man, but he feels very small inside. That is why he treats his wife so badly."

This is right, I think. But how does she know? The only time you hear them is when they're outside, when Mrs. Caros is hanging up the laundry or potting plants, and he sits behind her, smoking and telling her she's not worth much. But maybe Obaachan saw them out the window. Maybe that was it. Or maybe she's like me and things just come to her. Unexplainable.

She yawns. "Sleep is another world. Maybe a truer world."

But I'm not sleepy. I'm excited by the row of ants marching in a straight line across the bricks, the peeling bark on the birch, exposing every shade of brown that exists, the shadows of the leaves jangling on the lit pavement, and the spider waking and beginning her intricate weaving again, teasing out each spindly thread to its own destiny.

The Many Maynards

One of Mom's favorite phrases is "time flies." When I first heard the saying, I thought time *was* a fly, a small insect landing on a wall, with nowhere in particular to go. Mom explained that it meant time moved too fast, that only yesterday she was changing my diaper and Sally was doodling on the bathroom walls with Mom's lipstick. I nodded, but I still didn't get it. But Obaachan packs so much into our day that time does start to fly.

In the morning, we have a breakfast of *tamago*—sweet eggs on rice, wrapped with seaweed. I watch *Mr. Rogers* and *Barney*, then we play games outside or at the kitchen table. My favorite is Life, where you drive a car on the board and find a career, get married, buy a house, and have children. It makes the seemingly impossible task of *getting a life*, as Sally would say, as easy as twisting the spinner and moving your game piece. In reality, I'm afraid I never will *get a life*, that if I can't be like Sally and the other girls at school, I won't make friends, be invited to parties, find a career, get married, or have a family. All of those achievements would mean having to talk.

Life also amuses Obaachan, who finds in the board's instructions the very definition of being American. She giggles softly when she lands on the space that tells her she has twins or picks the card that gives her a mansion; she frowns when she has to pay the travel agent for a vacation, or the rock star for a concert.

After games, Obaachan teaches me to meditate. It is as simple as being a statue and as difficult as quieting your mind. At first, Obaachan has me close my eyes. She tells me to listen to my breath, to watch my thoughts float away like balloons, then to just be. She offers me a mantra: *Mu*. "In English, it translates to 'emptiness' or 'nothingness.' You can say it in your mind if your thoughts are wandering."

"*Mu*." I try out the word.

"It is the ability to make yourself disappear, so that God can appear." I can tell that Obaachan's God is different from the God in our church. Obaachan's God is a place, maybe even a feeling. The church's God is a person. He has rules and gets mad. If you're bad, he punishes you forever.

Later, when I try to explain *Mu* to Sally, she says, "Only

you would think that disappearing is a good thing." But what I can't explain is that in the emptiness of meditation I feel fuller than I ever have been, like I am a part of everything, down to the particles of light in the sky.

Obaachan also tells me about the history of Japan: the Kamakura Period and the legal codes based on Confucius, the wars with the Mongols and the battles for territory; the shoguns, who ruled for six hundred years; the dynasty of emperors and the samurai warriors who were at the top of the caste system.

She reads to me from her favorite book, *The Sound of the Mountain*, by Yasunari Kawabata. It is about an old man who hears the mountain calling to him. "When it is time to go, earth calls you back to her," she says, which gives me a bad feeling.

Then we have lunch. While Mom has won awards for her cooking, I prefer Obaachan's simple dishes of noodles, rice, miso soup, vegetables, or fried fish with ginger. In the afternoon, Obaachan rests and I play my cello or we listen to my Yo-Yo Ma CDs. I would like to be like Yo-Yo Ma, except I do not want to perform in front of people.

"Are you tired?" I ask Obaachan.

"Just my blood is tired."

So long as it is just her blood, I feel less worried.

With these full days, time does sprout wings and fly. September comes before I even notice it is August and I am startled to think that soon I'll be in the noisy, chopped-up days of school; an ant counting each movement of the clock, so that each minute takes an hour.

When the day comes, I am not cheered by my inheritance of Sally's clothes, which are pink and orange and loud and fit me too loosely, nor even by the new Hello Kitty backpack outfitted with sharp pencils in a matching case.

"Back to the pen," Sally says, sighing, as we approach the huge, blue brick building.

"Pen?" I ask. "Like writing?"

"No. Like *penitentiary*."

"What's that?"

"It's a jail. Doesn't this building look like a jail?"

"I don't feel good."

"What is it? Your stomach?"

"Yes."

"That's just butterflies."

"What if I throw up?"

"Don't be a 'fraidy cat, Lin. Or at least, don't let anyone know you are. A kid who smells like fear is an easy target. This isn't kindergarten. You can't be a baby forever."

"The bus smelled." In kindergarten Dad drove me.

"Yeah, but you get to ride with me!"

"It's too hot to go to school."

"It is hot. It's like fall broke its leg or something."

That gives me an idea. "My leg hurts. There's something wrong with it." I limp.

"That's very convenient." One of Mom's phrases. "You're starting to act like me. Come on. You don't want to make us late our first day. I promised myself that *this year* I'd stay out of the principal's office."

Around the big double doors is a mural of fish. The children and the humps of their backpacks swim into it.

"Do they call it a school because it's like a school of fish?" I ask Sally.

"Knucklehead." Sally takes my hand and drags me to the office where the lists of students and their teachers hang on the glass window.

"I wish I could stay with Obaachan," I tell her.

"Yeah, you and Grandma could be locked in the house for life and be perfectly happy. But you know, Lin, you gotta expand your universe a little. Oh-my-God." Her head snaps to the left. "Did you see him?"

"Who?"

"That was Walker Briggs. His parents yanked him out last year and put him in private school. Now he's back. He got in loads of trouble when he was here. He is the cutest boy in the school, and the richest, and the most daring."

"He just looked regular to me."

"If he's in my class, I'll just die."

"I don't like him." A loud buzz makes me jump. I *am* a 'fraidy cat.

"That's the first bell. Let's find out who your teacher is and I'll walk you to class." Sally pulls her finger down the list. "You have Mrs. Maynard. What is it with that name? There's, like, three of them in this school. Mrs. Maynard, first grade. Mr. Maynard, fourth grade; he used to be a sub. Yawn. If you want to be bored out of your gourd, listen to one of Maynard's lectures on history. To hear him go on, you'd think that Benjamin Franklin was God's first cousin or something. And Ms. Maynard. P.E. Nazi. She actually has tennis balls glued to the roof of her car. The car looks like some kind of insect. The many Maynards. Come on. The class is downstairs."

"What's a Nazi?"

"Never mind. You've got a few years before that pleasant piece of history is introduced."

"Is my Mrs. Maynard nice?"

"She's all right. She looks like a giraffe and acts like a drill sergeant. Don't ask me what that is. I got kicked out of her class for throwing a chair at her, but I doubt she'll hold it against *you*. I have to go. Remember, we're in the same school now. Don't be lame and embarrass me. You need to fit in."

"Okay."

"And try to make a friend for yourself."

"Obaachan's my friend."

"My point, exactly."

Tea Leaves

After three months at school, I still spend the day looking forward to going home, to the stretch of time from three to six when Obaachan and I can play games, talk, and meditate.

Finally, we have winter break. Sally and I come home to a table laid out with fresh fruit, sushi, tempura, and candies Obaachan makes from bean paste.

"How was your day, girls?" Obaachan asks.

"Fine, aside from the teachers, the classes, and the schoolwork." Sally grabs a diet Coke and a can of Pringles and heads for the computer, ignoring the feast.

"Are *you* enjoying school, Lin?" Obaachan peers at me.

"I guess." I lie, although compared to kindergarten, it is better. There is work at least, and we get to sit at our own desk, which makes it less noticeable that I don't have a friend.

A couple of girls did speak to me this week. In art, a girl complimented me on my painting of a sparrow. "Looks like it's going to fly," she said. But by the time I had pulled my voice into my mouth, she'd already moved back to her own easel. Irma asked to borrow a pencil from me. I gave it to her without a word; she never returned it. And at rehearsal for the holiday play, Edna Farrell changed places with me so I wouldn't have to stand in the front.

At least the kids aren't mean to me like they are to this one boy, Cole, who always does the opposite of what he's supposed to do. If Mrs. Maynard says "Come to the door," he stays in his seat. If she says "Sit," he climbs on the shelves. The other kids make faces at him and throw wadded paper. They imitate the thick way he speaks. Cole ignores them, but I know his feelings, as if they were my own. He feels like there's a plant inside of him that hasn't had any water, drooping, dying.

Matt Perino is one class over. I see him dashing out of the door every afternoon with the back of his hair sticking straight up. When *he* saw a boy making fun of Cole in the hall, he said, "Knock it off!" So at least there's one person to stick up for Cole.

The only kids from kindergarten who are in my class are Irma and Ahab, and they've stuck together just like they did then. Even to them, I am invisible.

"What did you do today?" Obaachan asks.

"We added numbers and learned about vowels. We made place mats out of woven paper. The teacher read us a story."

"What was it about?"

"A goose who lays golden eggs."

"Ah, I know a story about a goose."

"What was it?"

"It was a tale I heard when I was little and I always remembered it."

"Tell it to me."

"I told it to your mom when she was your age, and she couldn't sleep that night, so I'd better not. I will tell it to you when you're older. I promise."

"What was Mom like when she was my age?"

She chuckles. "She was like Sally, restless, wanting to be someone else, struggling to come out into the world like a lizard shedding skin. She was . . . attached."

"What does that mean?"

"Ah, inquisitive one. Attachment means having ideas of how things should be. And if things are not that way, you are unhappy. America is the land of attachment, I think."

"I don't understand."

"Let's see. Say you have some money. You go to the toy store. There is a big sale on toys. Everything is . . . uh . . . one cent. But the store is full of people crowding to get at the good toys."

"That would be fun."

"Would it really be fun? Would the people behave kindly to one another?"

"No. Maybe not. They might be pushing to get to what they wanted. They might be worried they won't find the toy they want."

"And would they be relaxed and calm? Would they be *sane?*"

"I guess not."

"That is attachment."

"I see."

"Yes. You do." She smiles. "Shall I make some tea?"

"Yes, please."

Obaachan doesn't use the tea bags like Mom does; she puts loose leaves in a small pot, lets it steep, then pours it into tiny cups. "Let's see what the leaves have to tell us." She turns her cup in a circle. The water swirls the leaves. "Ah, today, the leaves speak about you. They say you are a young duckling afraid to enter the water. The other ducklings are swimming away. You want to catch them, but you don't want to get your feet wet."

"What should I do? Plunge in?"

"Hmmmm." She swirls the cup again. "Time. In time, you will enter the water. Someday, you'll even like school."

"You think so?" *That's hard to believe.*

"Yes, but it will be a while," she says.

"It's just . . . I don't belong there." That's all I can really say. The shouts. The shoving. The chattering girls. And I know that this feeling, un-belonging, will be there in second grade and third and fourth.

"You will always swim in your own direction. That's a good thing. That takes strength. In the end, you will be the better for it."

"Yes?"

"But, it's hard now. I know. To be different. When I was your age I wanted more than anything to be like the other girls in my town. They all seemed prettier and happier. They laughed and played. When I was growing up, the girls did not go to school. Now it's different, of course. A much better time to be a girl. And you will do important work. Science, I think."

"I want to be a cellist like Yo-Yo Ma."

"You are very good at it."

"What about Sally? Do the leaves say anything about her?"

Obaachan sips her tea. "Here's a koan for Sally. A master pours a cup of tea for his student. The cup overflows, but the master keeps pouring. 'The tea is spilling,' the student shouts. 'You are like this cup,' the master replies, 'so full of yourself and your ideas of reality. You must make room to learn anything.' You see." Obaachan empties her cup in one gulp. "Sally's cup is so full of what she thinks she *should* be, that her true nature can't come to her. Still, I think . . . I'm sure she will find herself."

I peer into the tea. There are days when I hear voices in leaves, and music in the wind. Clouds swirl into promises. But when I try to see a message in the leaves, I only see specks of black, as if someone put a dirty shoe into a puddle. So I add sugar, snow falling through a green pool and dissolving.

"It will come," Obaachan says. "You will learn."

The tea tastes like the candies that I've long since eaten: sweet and bitter, and full of deep thoughts.

Food

In second grade, I receive a card in the mail, telling me which catechism teacher I will have. As soon as I open the envelope, two words come into my mind: Matt Perino. I half expect to see his name printed on the sheet of paper. "Sister April," I read aloud.

Sally comes in and grabs a cookie. "Mom's peanut butter cookies. Almost as good as a Big Mac. What are you reading?"

I hand her the card.

"Oh my God." Sally groans and collapses onto the floor, like the cookie has poisoned her. "Sister April, queen of the ruler."

I picture a queen on a throne, but that doesn't seem like a nun. "Why do you call her queen of the ruler?"

"Because she likes to hit the students' hands with rulers. Whack! It stings like crazy."

"Did you ever get hit?"

"Duh! Am I Sally O'Neil, or what?"

"How many times?"

"*Every* time. Once, it was for talking. Once, for wiggling in my seat. Once, I stuck my tongue out at her. That was worth it." Sally draws a picture of a nun on the card, ruler in hand, then she adds an arrow into her heart.

"I'm supposed to bring that with me."

"Oops."

"Why didn't you tell on her?"

"And let the parents know that I was getting into trouble? Not on your life. True, Mom and Dad don't hit, or punish much, but one look at Dad's disappointed puppy dog look puts me in a bad mood for days. You're just lucky Sister April got into trouble."

"What kind of trouble?"

"For the hitting. Some kid did have the guts to tell his mom. The mom complained to social services. Child abuse. It was a very big deal. It was even in the newspaper. Father Donnelly made her stop."

My heart races. "Are you sure she doesn't do it anymore?"

"I'm sure. And even if she did, can you imagine my goody-goody sister getting in trouble?"

"Yes." I nod. "I can."

Sally cracks up at that. "Don't worry; the only thing you'll be is bored. I personally challenge you to stay awake when she goes on and on in her droning voice. It's worse than church."

"I like church."

"You would. It's so pointless. And Mom makes out it's, like, the only place you can pray. But you can pray anywhere. You can pray on the toilet if you want to, while you're pooping."

"*Do* you pray?" It's hard to imagine.

"Sure. Everybody prays."

"What do you pray for?"

"For a house that's ours; for nicer clothes; for a laptop; a cell phone; to be prettier; for Walker Briggs to notice me; to be more popular; to get that outfit in the window of Limited Too."

"You're popular."

"Not enough. And when I remember, I pray for forgiveness and poor people, blah, blah, blah. But I usually don't remember. What do you pray for?"

"Nothing. Or maybe . . . that everything will stay the same."

"You are so weird!"

Dad drives me to the church in his pickup truck. There are tools under my feet: saws and sledgehammers, an orange hard hat. The smell of his cab—paint and turpentine—reminds me of the salon, of working and knowing your place in the world. Why, I wonder, if I know things about other people, do I never know anything about myself? Like what my future will be.

"I wish I'd just taken the side streets instead of this 'short-cut' of your mom's," Dad complains.

"Dad."

"What?"

"What do you pray about?"

"I don't pray, really. If I was going to pray, I'd pray that everything stays the same, that we're all healthy and happy like we are now."

Maybe I'm not that weird after all. "Obaachan says Mom didn't grow up Catholic."

"She converted to my religion when we got married, not that I asked her to. And she's taken to it like I never did."

"How come Mom never talks about growing up in Japan?"

"Maybe it wasn't that great for her."

"But you've told us lots of stories about visiting Ireland and about your mom and dad and stuff. So it's, like, we know more about you."

"Stories can be something that add to your life, like a garden and windows add to a house. You know my parents both died when you were a baby. They were in a car accident. My stories keep them alive for me. But some people feel trapped by their stories and they want to break free of them."

"Did your parents have red hair, like you?"

"Yep."

"Why don't we look like you?"

"Just lucky, I guess." He laughs.

I try to picture myself with curly red hair and blue eyes. If I looked like that, I would not be me. I would be a girl who talks loudly, like my dad does, whose eyes laugh, like his, who everyone likes.

But no. It's not just the red hair, the freckles, and blue eyes. That's too easy.

Because the girl who is like the one I imagine—loud, funny, confident, *American*—is one I know very well, and she looks Japanese: Sally. The most popular girl in school.

"Here we are. I think I just let you off at this roundabout."

"Sally says Sister April got in trouble for hitting kids with a ruler."

"Sally was pulling your leg, Lin. I went to elementary school with Sister April. Did you know that?"

"No."

"I doubt she remembers me. Hey, look, the police are here." He jokes, pulling in behind a squad car. "Better in front of me than behind me."

My heart pounds. "It's a boy from my kindergarten."

"Oh, yeah. I remember that kid. The one whose hair sticks up. What was his name?"

"Matt Perino."

Matt jumps out of the car, tosses a wave to his dad, and dashes up the steps. I get out of dad's truck and follow Matt, slowly. "Bye, kiddo," Dad calls after me. "Good luck."

SEP❧

The classroom is in the parish house, but to get there, we walk through the church, dipping our fingertips in holy water, and making the sign of the cross.

As I follow the other kids, I look at each painting of the Stations of the Cross: Jesus betrayed by Judas, dragged away by guards, his crucifixion and resurrection. *This is God*, I tell myself, but it's hard to understand, like translating Japanese. I can't figure how the sounds of one language match the meanings of another.

I prefer the statue of Mary with her open arms and palms up, as if she will give to anyone who asks. That makes more sense.

Aside from Matt, there are several kids from my school: Mary Stevens, Cora, and Irma.

While some of the nuns wear gray skirts and white blouses, Sister April wears a traditional habit, black and floor length. She has dark brown eyes and fierce black eyebrows.

She tells us to fold our hands and place them on the Bibles in front of us, then she talks about nuns, the different kinds of things they do. She only looks at the girls. It's like she can see us in a row marching toward the convent.

In the old days, she says, there were nuns who bled from their hands out of sympathy with Christ. There was a nun who dreamed music then awoke to compose it, even though she never played an instrument.

Even though it's cold outside, the room is boiling. I can't

imagine wearing a heavy black dress in here. "A nun's life is devoted to prayer and good works, to turning inward to the spirit . . ."

After a day in the classroom, my eyelids are droopy. I feel like I'm floating, and as I drowse, a story unfolds like a movie in my mind. I see a young woman sitting at a wooden table by herself. She is thin, maybe fourteen or fifteen, but I know it is Sister April. The house is empty and silent. There is a knock at the door. She stands, picks up a suitcase, and moves toward it. I am filled with the sadness that was hers.

Whack. My head jerks up. I look around to see whose hand was hit with the ruler. The girl in front of me picks up her Bible, which has dropped to the floor. "Sorry."

Sister April manages a small smile. "At least it woke some of us up." She looks at me.

Matt raises his hand. "Why do nuns take a vow of poverty?"

"Because suffering is the shortest path to the heart of God. There is a saying, 'Even when the door of God is closed, his window is open to tears.' In suffering, we meet God."

"But can't you meet God through joy?" Matt asks.

Sister April folds her arms. "Not really. Although it's joy to suffer. Yes, I think Jesus had a joyful suffering."

His hand shoots up again.

"You don't have to raise your hand every five seconds. We are in conversation. You may speak."

"Then why do we sing?"

"What?"

"Why do we sing in church if not out of joy?"

"It's a form of prayer. And prayer is a brief release from the torment we experience, which is Christ's torment."

"Do you mean suffering that people bring onto themselves, like you deciding to be poor and live with those other nuns and eat bad food? Or suffering that happens to people without their choice, like war? I mean . . . which is the better suffering?"

"The food isn't that bad."

"It's not good. That's for sure. My aunt is a nun at St. Christopher's and I ate with them. The food was all starchy and boring. The meat looked and tasted like a gray sponge. The pasta was overcooked. The salad was iceberg lettuce." He grimaces. "There were no spices, no oregano or rosemary or garlic. I mean, how come the priests get to live in the big house? Why do they get good meals and wine and a housekeeper and fancy robes? Father Price eats lamb and steak every night."

"How do you know?"

"I *know*," he says in a way that is absolutely convincing.

"Of what matter is food to the spirit? It is a better person who eats gruel and mortifies the flesh than one who indulges and lives for pleasure."

"If God made good food," Matt says loudly, "like melon, eggplant, Asiago cheese, cannelloni, and garlic, isn't it a sin not to enjoy it?"

"Why do you care so much about food, anyway, Mr. Perino? What's the *big deal?*"

Matt looks at Sister April like she's just asked the stupidest question in the world, like, Why are you a boy? "Because I'm Italian!"

"Well," she snaps. "That explains everything. Class dismissed."

On the way out, the other boys slap Matt on the back and congratulate him on upsetting Sister April and getting us released early.

"But I didn't get my questions answered." He nods to me. "Don't you wonder about these things? I mean, how do you make sense of it all?"

I want to tell him that maybe we don't have to make sense of it. The Virgin Birth. Christ's mortification. God as a parent who allows his son to suffer. Those stories are like the koans Obaachan tells. You meditate on them, let them flow through you. And then, maybe, you understand. But it can't be explained in words, any more than you could explain a feeling, or a piece of music.

"Don't ask *her*." Mary Stevens pulls her eyes to make them thin. "She's Chinese. She doesn't even speak English."

"Yes she does," Matt says. "She just doesn't speak it very loud."

Goldfish

In the winter, two important things happen. First, Sally and Marigold Strauss have a split. It is because of Walker Briggs. Marigold insists that Walker loves her. She can tell by the way Walker looks away whenever he passes her, as if the sight of her puts him into a state of "agonized longing."

Sally, though, insists that Walker loves *her*. Someone has left a goldfish in a plastic bag against her locker. "Everyone knows that Walker's parents own a chain of pet stores," she brags to Marigold.

"Then he would give you something more interesting than a *goldfish*. God! He would give you something exotic: a guppy, at least, for God's sake. Besides, what happened to the goldfish?"

Sally looks at the floor. She'd been so happy when she brought the goldfish home. She had pulled out one of Mom's casserole dishes, filled it with water, then carefully spilled the little fish out of its plastic bag. "What are you going to call it?" I asked.

"Walker. Of course."

All day she watched the fish swim circles. "He even moves like Walker," Sally said. "He's so sure of himself."

The last time I'd seen Walker Briggs, he was coming out of the boys' room. I *guess* he looked sure of himself. The tail of his shirt was sticking through where he'd zipped it in. He stopped to pick his nose. He gave me a bad feeling.

Now, if there was a boy who was nice-looking, it was Matt Perino. I wanted to point that out to Sally, but I was afraid she'd make fun of me.

When Mom came home, Sally got in trouble for bringing a pet home without asking, and worse, using Mom's casserole dish. But Dad took Sally to a pet store. They got fish food and a proper bowl.

Sally talked to the fish when she fed it like she was casting a spell. "Here, Walker. Look who feeds you. The one who feeds you, needs you."

In the middle of the night, though, I woke up to a scream. Sally had her light on and she was clutching the fishbowl. "What's wrong?" I asked.

"He's floating at the top like a dead fish," she cried.

I peered in, too sleepy to be tactful. "He *is* a dead fish."

For two days, Sally hardly said a word. She didn't go online and check her e-mail, or listen to music on her headphones. She mourned that fish like it was a person.

Marigold repeats the question. "I said, 'What happened to the fish?'"

"It died," Sally snaps. "And my dad flushed it down the toilet like a wad of paper."

"Exactly."

Sally taps her foot like Mom. Her face gets red. "You know why Walker looks away when he passes you. Because he thinks you're gross. If you're interested in someone, you look at them! You don't look away."

"I want my American Girl dolls back!" Marigold bursts into tears.

"I want my hula skirt back!"

Sally is getting the worse deal. The American Girl dolls are beautiful and old-fashioned like our house. They cost a hundred dollars each. Sally could never have one, not even for her birthday, but Marigold, who has several, allowed the Samantha and Molly dolls to visit Sally since last summer. The hula skirt had been dragged from the dollar bin at the Party Store at a post-Halloween sale.

After that day, Marigold always walks on the other side of the street. She turns her face away when she passes our house.

Even her mom, Daisy, stops saying hello to my mom when they run into each other at the school or store.

The second thing that happens is that Obaachan finally leaves the house. This winter is the worst ever. The ground is so frozen your shoes make a cracking sound with every step. Your eyelashes freeze. Cars skid off the road. Tree limbs snap from the weight of ice.

The small cough that Obaachan has had since fall turns into a constant hacking. No amount of ginger tea and honey will make it go away.

"You need to go to the doctor," Mom demands at breakfast.

"I will be fine. It's just the weather. It is too dry inside my chest."

"I am not ready to plan your funeral. You are going."

"I will decide when my funeral is. Of that I can promise you."

"You always were so stubborn. Even when I was little and I wanted to play with Toshiko. You wouldn't let me even talk to her."

"Her father was a war criminal. And the family had fleas."

"The *dog* had fleas!" Mom checks her watch. "Oh, I'm late. My first appointment is in ten minutes."

"Don't worry. She's not showing up. A house makes her not come."

"'A house makes her not come'? What does it do? Grab her by the leg and hang on to her?"

"Check your messages, Mayumi chan."

"Call me Marge," Mom says drily, but she goes to check her messages anyway.

"Grandma," Sally says through a mouth full of cornflakes. "You're keeping us all up at night with that cough."

"Oh." Obaachan seems startled. "You can hear it when you're sleeping?"

"*Trying* to sleep."

"I didn't realize it was disturbing you all. I'm so sorry."

"Whatever. It's not like it's a big deal."

Obaachan gets up stiffly and goes into her room.

Sally rolls her eyes. "I wasn't trying to make a big deal about it."

Dad bustles in. "Have you seen my newspaper?"

"Why do you call it *your* newspaper?" Sally says. "It comes to everyone."

"Because I'm the only one who reads it."

"That's all you ever do."

"Where is it, Sally?"

"I had to cut some things out for current events."

"This morning?"

"*Buffy the Vampire Slayer* was on last night. You don't expect me to miss that for homework?" She pulls the paper out from under the table. Squares have been cut out of the front page.

"Great. Fine. I'll buy one at Cumby's. How you doing, kiddo?" Dad pats my head.

"Fine."

"Miss Perfect," Sally snipes.

"If you two want to ride in the Dad Mobile instead of the bus, I'm going past the school."

"Yay," I say. I hate the loud, smelly bus.

"Not me. I wouldn't be caught dead in that truck. Why can't you get an SUV like everyone else?"

"I don't want to be like everyone else, Sally. You haven't figured that out yet?"

"Who do you want to be like, then? Bill Clinton?"

Dad gives her a dirty look. Bill Clinton used to be his hero, but lately Dad doesn't even like his name mentioned. "The Dalai Lama."

"Dream on."

"You'd better hustle, Sally, if you want to catch the bus."

"Get lost, Sally, is what you mean. And who thought up the lame name of Sally anyway?"

"It was my mother's name." Dad glares at her.

Sally gathers up her things and rushes out. Dad peers at the parts of the paper left.

"Is Obaachan really sick?" I ask.

"Huh?" He looks up.

"Why doesn't she want to go to the doctor?"

"She doesn't like Western medicine."

"What's wrong with her?"

"We'll take her to the doctor. Don't worry."

"Why don't Mom and Obaachan get along?"

"Sometimes mothers and daughters don't," he explains.

"The mom still views the child as a child, even after she's grown. But relationships have to change with time. It's hard. Like I can't imagine you a grown-up who doesn't have time for me."

I smile. "I'll always have time for you."

"Promise?"

"Yes. Dad?"

"Huh?"

"You said you knew Sister April, back in school?"

"She lived with her grandmother just down the street from here. In high school, her grandmother died. After that she joined the convent."

"Oh."

Mom comes in, the phone still in her hand. "She did cancel. She and her fiancé are making an offer on a house. I can take the girls to school."

Obaachan comes in wearing the kimono she wore the first day she arrived. "Daughter," she says. "I will go to the doctor."

"Not dressed like that," Mom says.

Red Face

That day when we come home from school, the house is empty. I am used to Obaachan at the door, the elaborate snack she will have laid out on the table, our games and talk. "Obaachan's gone!" I tell Sally.

"Maybe she went to the doctor."

"That's right. She did."

"God, I was so embarrassed when she overreacted this morning."

"That wasn't very polite."

"Get a life."

"Do you think she'll be all right?"

"Sure. It's just a cough." Sally turns on the TV with the

sound down, puts her Walkman on, and sits at the computer. "Oh my God!" she says loudly, "I've got thirty e-mails."

I sit on the couch a few minutes and stare at the TV, a music video with Madonna. Then I go to the kitchen and try to meditate, but thoughts keep racing through my mind. I think about Obaachan. Since she came, it feels like a missing puzzle piece being added to our lives, completing the picture. I think about the pink invitations passed through my classroom. When Sandy Howell gave me one, I thought it was for me. "Pass it back, before Mrs. Holmes catches us," she whispered. I passed it to Irma. By the end of class, it seemed like every girl had a pink envelope except me. Then I think about another note, one that has been sent home that says I should skip third grade.

Maybe it is because I miss Obaachan that I do it. I tiptoe down the hall to my old room and quietly open the door.

The shades are down. The room is dark. I turn on the light, and close the door behind me.

My room is unrecognizable. In the corner where my toy box used to be, there's a low wooden shelf with three statues on it: a man with a fat belly, a tiger, and a face that is half woman–half sun. Surrounding it are candles, incense, and a small bowl of tangerines.

The closet doors are covered with posters of mountains and waterfalls. On the high shelf are teapots, two identical wooden boxes, a vase, a stone that looks like white marble, and figures made of folded paper: a crane, a tall building, an elephant, a lady, a man and child holding hands. Covering the wall near the bed is a red silk hanging with a painted black circle. Something about that circle keeps me looking for a long time. It's imperfect, the lines don't quite connect, but it seems truer than the usual circle.

I open the closet. A kimono hangs there, one I haven't seen: blue, with silver lines shooting across it like falling stars. On the closet shelf are wooden shoes.

I am in Japan.

I am about to close the closet door when I see a bigger box, too high for me to reach. A word is printed on it, in black letters: H I R O S H I M A.

My face gets very red when I'm embarrassed, which happens often. I am embarrassed when someone speaks to me and I can't get my voice to answer. I am embarrassed when Mrs. Holmes calls on everyone but me. I am embarrassed when I see the words I LOVE WALKER BRIGGS, on a bathroom door and recognize Sally's handwriting.

But nothing matches the embarrassment I feel when I hear the footsteps on the stairs and Obaachan's cough. My face feels like flames are flashing inside my skin.

I rush into the kitchen, pour a bowl of cereal, and pretend to eat.

"Come into the kitchen and sit down, Mom. I'll make you some tea." Mom comes in and puts the kettle on. She pulls out a bottle from a white bag. "You're supposed to take this with food. I'll make an omelet."

"Just a little miso broth, Mayumi chan." Obaachan enters and sits across from me.

I push the cereal box in front of me and read the list of ingredients and added vitamins.

Obaachan's gaze is like an X-ray through the box. Sweat forms on my forehead, as if my hair is crying.

"Lin," Mom says. "I didn't know you were even here. You're quiet as a mouse. Did you say hello to your grandma?"

"Hello," I whisper.

"How did you pass your afternoon?" Obaachan says.

"I didn't finish my homework." I peer up. Her eyes hold mine for a second, then I pull away. "I'd better go do it."

All week, I avoid Obaachan. Instead of sitting with her and talking, I pretend I have a project or a report, that my teacher has become very vigorous with her assignments.

At dinner, I keep my eyes focused on my plate, the food that I push around to make Mom think I am eating.

"Sally, I thought you might want to take that cheerleading class," Mom says. "It's at the country club, but you don't have to be a member. I could drop you on the way to my chocolate-making class and pick you up on my way back. You'd have to wait fifteen minutes."

"Cheerleading is lame," Sally says. "Everything that used to be cool is lame. Why don't we ever eat out? I want a Big Mac in the worst possible way."

"The word *lame* is lame," Dad points out.

"Yoko's daughter is having a baby," Obaachan announces.

"Kana?" Mom says. "How nice. She must be at least thirty-five."

"Twins."

"Twins!" Dad says. "What a handful."

"Well, you always said Kana knew how to do things right. Didn't you, Mom?" Mom's foot taps under the table.

"I don't remember saying such a thing."

"Kana could do no wrong."

"Lin, eat your peas," Dad says.

"She doesn't eat anything," Sally says. "She's a stick."

"Eat," Mom says.

I lift the fork to my mouth.

"Dad, did you hear that the school wants Lin to skip third grade?" Sally asks.

"She is a very smart girl," Obaachan says.

My face burns.

"Yeah, Miss Perfect Girl Genius. Well, you're not gonna let that happen, are you? 'Cause it would be really bad for her. She's already the smallest one in her class. I mean, there are social considerations that are more important than schoolwork."

"Social considerations," Dad repeats. "Well put."

"She might be made fun of. Now she's just ignored."

"Sally!" Mom scolds.

"Lin's just studious. Right, kiddo?" Dad pats my head.

All eyes are on me. They expect an answer. I count the peas left on my plate. There are eighteen.

"Do you want to skip a grade?" Mom asks. "The work would be more interesting for you."

I would love to get through school more quickly, but like Sally says, at least I'm not made fun of. My classmates are familiar to me, even if I'm invisible to them. "No."

"You sure?"

"Yes."

"Decided," Dad says. "We don't really want you to grow up faster, to be out of the house a year earlier, anyway."

"Oh," Mom groans. "Time flies. I can't stand it."

"Remember when Lin thought that time *was* a fly," Sally says. Everyone laughs. Except Obaachan. Her eyes just stay on me, like two empty cups, waiting to be filled with green tea.

What We Carry

On Friday, Sally doesn't take the bus home with me, but goes to Molly's house. Because of Marigold's disappearance, Molly has been reinstated. It is not a good thing for me. Marigold was like her name: bright and cheerful. She let me join when they did makeovers or let me play a game with them when they needed three players.

But if I ask to play now, Molly's answer is always the same: "Get lost, pest."

"Yeah, get lost, Lin," Sally says. Sally is like that lizard that changes color to whatever it is near, a chameleon. With Marigold, Sally was friendlier, laughed more, said *God* about everything. With Molly, she acts like she's twenty instead of ten. At school, Sally hangs out with a whole bunch of girls. They all wear pink and imitate the girls on the Disney Channel.

I am so surprised when I get off the bus to see Obaachan waiting for me at the stop that I forget to look down.

"Your mother asked me to meet you. She didn't want you to walk alone. Now that I have left the house once, she expects me to do it every day."

I nod and wonder if it was very hard, leaving the house by herself, or was it something good, like going to the doctor and getting better.

"There were two monks," she says as we walk, "standing by a river. There had been a storm and the river was high, spilling over its banks. A beautiful girl came to them, dressed in an elegant kimono, and she was crying. 'What is wrong?' the first monk asked. 'I can't get across to go home,' the girl answered. Without a moment's hesitation, the first monk picked her up and carried her across the river, holding her high so that her kimono would not be spoiled. Then he crossed back to his friend. The monks continued their travels, but for the rest of the day, the second monk wouldn't speak to the first. Finally, after supper, the first monk asked the second what was wrong. 'We are monks. We are not to associate with women, and yet you carried that girl in your arms.' The first monk smiled. 'I left the girl on the other side of the river,' he said. 'Why are you still carrying her?'"

I am used to Obaachan's koans. I know they don't need an answer. Still, I think hard. It was kind that the first monk carried the girl. It was the right thing to do, to help another in distress.

Obaachan stops on the sidewalk and bends close to me. "I forgive you for going into my room. I am not carrying that."

Tears boil up into my eyes.

"I would have invited you in if I'd known you were curious."

Sometimes, if you pull on a rubber band, it snaps. That is how my heart feels, surging with relief, blood flowing through it again. "Like George?" I say.

"Yes. Besides, it is *your* room. I am only borrowing it for a while."

"You're not going back to Japan, are you?"

"No. I will never see Japan again. I am certain of that."

"Girls! Lovely ladies!" Mr. Caros calls from the mailbox in front of our house. "Where have you been on such a gloomy day?"

"Just the bus stop," Obaachan says. "I'm not very adventurous."

"Well, there are external adventures, and internal adventures." He taps his head.

"Very wise," Obaachan says. "A man of such wisdom and a

love for fine things like opera, that is a man who knows that what is most precious to one in his life, is what one should honor most and treat best."

Mr. Caros blushes.

"You will do that," she instructs.

"Oh, yes. Of course."

"And to answer your other question, I would use a spray of soap and water for the mold on the houseplants."

As we head up the stairs to our apartment, Mr. Caros calls after us. "But I didn't ask yet!"

Obaachan takes the same path that I took into her room, going first to the little shelf and carpet. "This is my *Kami-Dana*, a shelf of the gods. This is the Buddha." She points to the round man. "He started out in a very wealthy family but was moved by the suffering of the poor and the sick. *Compassion* was the beginning of Buddhism and is its end result. These others are the gods of the Shinto faith. I meditate here and offer my prayers. These are origami figures. They are made of folded paper, a Shinto art. I should teach you. This stone belonged to your grandfather. He found it when he was walking in the mountains as a boy. He felt it had magic power, that it had kept him from harm that had fallen on others."

"What is that?" I point to the painted circle.

"Ah, you would notice that. That is *Enso*, which means 'circle.' It has many meanings: 'empty cup,' 'turning wheel,' 'eye of Buddha,' 'circle of life.' It is a symbol of Zen Buddhism and the true nature of enlightenment, both the visible and the hidden. And this"—she points to the posters—"is Mount Nantai and Kegon Waterfall. We went after we were married. You see, there is no mystery here."

But there is still a mystery, and so I ask, "Obaachan, what is HIROSHIMA?"

A Dying Cat

May is my least favorite month. For one thing, it's supposed to be spring, but it's usually cold. For another, the annual cello recital occurs. Each year, I have to talk my way out of it. Once it's over, Ms. Nga goes on and on about how nice it would have been if her best student had bothered to play.

"The cello is an overlooked instrument," Miss Nga is lecturing me. "The whiny violin gets all the attention; the pounding piano. This is because the cello gives voice to sadness, longing, and loneliness. You are my best student because you understand this. Therefore, you will do *two* songs at the recital." She says this like she's doing me a favor.

"I don't *do* the recital, Ms. Nga. Remember? My hands will freeze like icebergs and I'll embarrass you."

"I don't train my students to play for themselves. It will be fine. You'll just apply yourself to it . . ."

Mom defends me. "Lin needs to take things at her own pace."

"She is a virtuoso, my best student ever. She *must* play in public. Otherwise, all of this work is for nothing. If she doesn't play, I don't see any reason to continue her lessons."

Mom looks startled. "Well, I guess it will help her prepare for Communion."

Sally makes dying cat sounds.

"Stop that!" Mom scolds.

After Ms. Nga leaves, I try to enlist Dad into making some excuse for me.

He shakes his head. "It's time to come out a little, kiddo."

Even Obaachan agrees that I should play for an audience, although her instructions are different from Ms. Nga's. "Meditate on the music and you will forget the audience."

Meditation is the very opposite of "applying myself" or making an effort. It is about *not* trying and allowing things to come to you.

And since I've been meditating, things do come to me. Like I go to bed knowing what the weather will be the next day, so I can lay out my clothes. I can feel it if a test will be postponed, or easy or hard. My talent for knowing what someone will say increases, and I also understand how they feel. It's said that we use only 10 percent of our brains. Maybe meditation gives a nudge to that percentage. That's the only way I can explain it.

I also dream more vividly, then carry the dreams with me all day like a secret life. I dream that I am flying above the city of Providence like an angel. I dream of other families who have lived in this house. When I wake up, I can almost hear the walls breathe their names, and picture them moving through the rooms: a man opening a window, a woman walking through the hall in a long dress, a little boy playing with jacks. I wonder, Will the house remember us when we're gone, too? Will the scent of Mom's brownies float through the hall, or Obaachan's incense?

Sometimes my dreams actually happen. Like I dreamed that my teacher was hurt. That morning the principal said she'd been in a car accident and would be out for a few weeks. I dreamed a man in a suit came to our house. The next morning, there was a knock at the door. "Jehovah's Witness." Dad peeked out the window. "Don't answer." The man left pamphlets saying that the world would end.

There are two dreams I keep having over. In one, I'm in the white smock walking down corridors. In the other, there's a woman with red hair. She stands in a green field waving to me. As I walk toward her, the red hair on her head turns completely white.

❧

The night before my cello recital, though, I have a nightmare. I am walking to the stage in my white dress. The audience is there, their faces hard, like Cole's when the kids make fun of him. When I draw my bow across the strings, a yowling sound is emitted from my instrument, the sound of cats fighting, screaming, and dying.

In the morning, I sit at the table with my arms crossed. Sally is looking over Dad's shoulder while he reads the paper. "Sally, what are you doing?"

"Trying to read the paper."

"Since when are you interested in the news?"

"Saint Clinton is in hot water."

"That's X-rated." Dad shoves the paper into the recycling bin.

"It's always a woman," Sally says.

"Did you know that since you started middle school, you're a little hard to take first thing in the morning." Dad finally looks at me. "What's the matter?"

"Sally gave me bad dreams."

"Really?" Sally says. "I didn't think people could *give* each other dreams."

"What did you dream?" Dad shoves toast at me. I keep my arms folded.

"I dreamed that my cello sounded like a cat."

Sally erupts into giggles. "Oh, that is good. That is so hilarious."

"Be nice," Dad says.

"What if it really happens?" I ask.

"It won't. Sally, tell her it won't happen."

"It won't," Sally says. "When have you ever done *anything* that isn't *perfect?*"

The whole day, I'm in the worst mood of my life. I won't play games or talk to anyone. I can't eat. The recital is at two o'clock. At one, Mom tells me I should be dressed. I put my dress on as slowly as possible. It's too big so it will fit for Communion, too.

Once we are there, Ms. Nga pulls me away from my family and I have to sit in a chair *right on the stage.* I feel so angry at her for making me do this that I hope my bow strings do sound like a dying cat. That will show her.

When Ms. Nga gets up to speak to the audience, her foot slips on a piece of sheet music someone has dropped, and she lands on one knee. I look up. Her face is as red as mine probably is. Her voice quivers as she recovers, then she speaks in her slow accented voice, about how hard the children have worked. When I realize that she is as scared as I am, my anger melts and I want to do well for her.

I am first so I can get it over with. She calls my name. I stand, then cross to the chair at the center of the stage. I place my music and lift my bow. I focus on a spot in front of me on the floor: *Mu, Mu, Mu.* Then I smile to myself when I realize what word begins with *Mu: music.*

Ms. Nga sounds the piano key, the first note of the accompaniment. But I don't *try* like she's told me to; I let the music come to me, so that I am *Mu* and music, one with the notes, the motion of my hands.

I begin with Bach's Suite no. 1, a piece that reminds me of children dancing. Then I go right to my favorite piece, Fauré's Elégie. An elegy is a poem or a song for the dead. It was Fauré's first composition for cello. When I play it I feel like I am expressing all the sadness in the world, that I am telling Fauré himself that even though he became deaf and sad in later years, he is still heard now.

It is over so quickly that I am convinced I missed notes. But Ms. Nga is beaming at me. The audience is clapping. Mom, Dad, and Sally are crying and laughing at the same time. Obaachan's hands are to her lips like a prayer.

I take my bow.

I have spoken for Bach and for Fauré.

And the cello has spoken for me.

ENSO

Summer, 2000

The Secret

·

At 8:15 A.M. on August 6, 1945, at the end of a world war that had lasted six years, the atomic bomb was dropped on Hiroshima.

Obaachan was there. She was fifteen years old. She'd moved from Kyoto to Hiroshima with her mother only a month before, after her father died in the war. They ran a small tea shop, two tables on the street in front of their house, and sold sweets they had made on their stove.

For weeks, Obaachan had dreamed of piles of sticks, of burning rubbish, and a snowstorm made of ash. The whine of a mosquito became, in dreams, the buzz of a plane. Thunder sounded like a bomb.

Still, when it happened, she was unprepared, washing clothes in the Kyobashi River like it was any other day. A boy she liked had stolen her mother's dress from the water and was dancing with it, holding it against him, just out of her reach. She was grabbing for it and hollering at him that he'd better give it back.

She didn't remember hearing anything, just a silence more quiet than prayer. Then the light.

"What did it look like?" I ask.

"Like the sun had crashed into the earth and exploded into flames. Like a volcano erupting in the sky. A building in the distance became a skeleton of ash. Birds and objects rained from the sky. My mother's dress floated away from me on the river. I knew then that she was gone. The dream I'd had didn't help *prevent* anything."

My great-grandmother. "She died?"

"Yes."

"What happened to the boy?"

"I don't know. He was there and then not, like our lives. That's what they called it."

"What?"

"The bomb. They called it Little Boy. And years later, when I knew I was having a child, I prayed that it would be a girl, so I wouldn't have to think those words."

"But why did it happen?"

"In war, there is never any reason; there is only attachment and ego and power. That is the cause of war and of all suffering."

She tells me this on August 14, a day commemorating the surrender of the Japanese following the atomic bombing of Hiroshima and Nagasaki. We are walking by the river, where on summer weekends lit fires float in the water.

I have waited two years for her to explain. She tells me now because I am old enough to understand the circular path of history, the dark and light side of human beings like the very cycle of night and day. She tells me because I have read Sally's history textbook and learned about other fires in the same war: ovens that whole families were forced into because of their religion.

And Obaachan talks about her life with my grandfather and my mother in Tokyo, how Mom didn't want to hear about the war, or about the emperor, who was thought to be God, but whose voice when he conceded defeat to the United States sounded as frail as rice paper. Mom wanted only to learn about the Americans, and how instead of "slaughtering everyone," as Obaachan had been told they would, they had driven through the streets of Japan in their tanks, tossing candy to children. They delivered boxes of food from the same planes that had once dropped bombs.

Mom wanted to learn English and travel.

She wanted to be American.

She sang songs by Elvis Presley and wore her skirt too short. After Mom married my dad and moved to America,

Obaachan could still hear "Love Me Tender" in the shower, and "Jailhouse Rock" in the hall. She could smell the chemical scent of European perfume on the sheets and pillows, like flowers dipped in formaldehyde.

The trees are rustling their leaves. Shadows flicker on the sidewalk. The sky is the kind of blue that Dad says you can only see in New England, clear as the purest water.

And in that sky, I do see it all: the flames, the river, my great-grandmother's dress floating away, my Obaachan a fifteen-year-old girl, wandering the streets alone through burning houses and bodies.

Then I know something about time, that it, too, is a river. That it surrounds like water.

And I wade into it.

I Will Not Always Be Here

*O*nce Obaachan tells me the story of Hiroshima, I need to know more. It is like a dessert I can't stop eating. I am hungry for the past.

I check out books at the library and read more about the bombing: the buildings that were there and then not, the people who disintegrated instantly, leaving their shadows on the sidewalk, the fabric designs on the women's dresses that scorched onto their skin, creating embeddings of flowers and winding vines and geometric patterns.

I read of the thick foliage that erupted from the rubble, "atomic" flowers and vines, the mutations of plants and insects; strange life out of death.

There were seven Catholic priests from Germany. Their church was destroyed, but their house was left standing. None were injured or developed the illnesses associated with radiation: the anemia and cancers that would visit even the children of survivors, which makes me worry about my mom. The priests credited the miracle to the beads of the rosary, their habit of prayer.

Then there were the Hiroshima Maidens, women whose faces were disfigured by the bomb. Ten years after the war, they came to America to be operated on. They became celebrities here.

Now, sometimes, I have a nightmare that I am running down burning streets calling for my mother. I stop everyone I see and ask the question of all history: *How can we do this to one another?*

No one answers me, though; they just point into the distance, like the answer is far away and I have to keep chasing it.

When Obaachan and I take our daily walks by the river, or along Benefit Street, where the night-colored buildings have the names of their owners and the dates they were built, I ask questions. "How did you survive without your mother?" I can't imagine being without my mother.

"At first, I was in shock. I tried to find someone to help me. Instead, I kept finding those *I* needed to help: a burned woman, a man crushed by a fallen shed, a lost child. Eventually, I worked in a building where the wounded were taken, trying to hand out what little medicine there was, bandaging wounds. There is a saying. 'Nothing is more whole than a broken heart.' It sounds strange, but it can be true. Before the disaster, I was like any young girl: vain, attached. I worried that the other girls had nicer clothes than me. I wondered if I was pretty. After, my only thought was how I could help others. And when I did, my heart was filled, and I forgot about myself and my own sadness. I think this is what you will do. Help others." She smiles. "And in this way, you will forget about your *shyness*."

My throat swells. I will never forget my shyness. "Then what did you do?"

"I left Hiroshima, finally. The doctor at the hospital where I worked became ill, and he went to Tokyo for treatment. He allowed me to accompany him and I found work there, in a dress factory. But I missed working in a hospital. I would have liked to be a nurse."

"Why did you leave Hiroshima?"

"Because of the shame. Those who survived the bomb were known as Hibakusha. To be a Hibakusha was to be ashamed. To be treated with shame. Those with the scars from the bomb—keloids they were called—could not hide that they were Hibakusha."

"But it wasn't their fault."

"To be a victim is to feel it is your fault. But I didn't have visible scars. Many also left because they said the ground was still poisonous, which it was. Others left because of the river. It was said that the ghosts of the dead hovered like lost clouds over the water, calling out the names of their loved ones."

"Did you see ghosts?"

"I never returned to the river. After the war, Japan became a country of peace. We never invaded or attacked anyone again. That is remarkable. A whole way of being, centuries of warrior behavior, changed completely. The hunger we had for territory transformed into an appetite for peace. This was the good that came from the war for Japan. And I met your grandfather in Tokyo and my friend Shizuko. It was two years before I realized that your grandfather was also Hibakusha."

"You didn't tell each other?"

"No. But one day, he found my box, the one you asked me about."

"What is in it?"

"The ashes of Hiroshima. I took them to remember my mother, hoping that maybe some bit of her was in there. And now your grandfather's ashes are in there, too. Hiroshima has become a beautiful city. There is a Peace Museum and monuments." She stops in front of a clothing shop and looks at a pink coat hanging in the window. "Time now for the present."

I try to think of the present. It is never very exciting, except that Ms. Nga has recommended me for a private school where she leads the orchestra. I was accepted to the school, but my parents are waiting to hear whether I will receive a scholarship. If I don't, I will not be able to go.

"Do you think I'll go to the new school?" I ask Obaachan.

"You are full of questions today. This must be the year of talking. Yes. You will. I am certain."

How are you certain? I want to ask, even though I know the answer. When things come to you in the center of your being, you know they are true.

"I hope it's nice there."

"Are you worried?"

"It's just . . . I'm used to my school. People leave me alone."

"It is time, I think, for you to *not* be left alone."

"But what if the kids at the new school aren't nice?"

She sighs. "I was very frightened to come here. I could barely get myself onto the plane. I think that if there was a slide down through the sky, back to Japan, I would have taken it. Like that one in the playground you used to like to go down."

"Is that why you stayed in your room?"

"I was tired, and once I got here I realized that I would never return to Japan and had sadness. I hadn't considered that. I had thought of this as a visit. But I walked into your apartment and realized that this would be my final place. I would not again see my country or Shizuko. But, would I give up this wonderful time with you and Sally?" She shakes her head. "Never."

The words *final place* give me a chill. "How old are you, Obaachan?"

She laughs. "Younger than the wind. Older than your mother."

But I know that she was fifteen in 1945. I do the math in my head. "You are seventy," I say.

"Am I? Yes. A new century."

"Remember how everyone thought the computers would shut down?"

"Yes, but since I know nothing of computers, I didn't understand."

"Computers are easy. If you learn to use one, you could e-mail Shizuko every day."

"I'm too old a horse."

"A horse?"

"To learn new tricks."

I smile.

"What? Did I get it wrong?"

It would be impolite to answer. "You must miss her."

"I speak to her every day at the same time. We have wonderful conversations. This morning, she told me of an old woman who came for a potion to make her husband love her, but Shizuko was able to show her that she was better off without her husband, that another love would arrive if she would let go. Shizuko told her, 'Drop like a petal and the wind will carry you.'"

"Did you talk on the phone?"

Obaachan taps her head. "Thoughts are just as loud as words and they travel faster. That's how well we know each other. Let's go in."

"Here?"

"Such a pretty coat would look so nice on you."

The idea of having a gift makes me feel shy. I've never seen Obaachan buy anything, ever. I follow her into the shop. "Let's get something for Sally."

"But she is only wearing black these days," Obaachan says.

I try on the coat. It is a rich material and fits me perfectly. The price tag says two hundred dollars. "It's too much," I say, wanting the coat.

Obaachan smiles. She pulls out her wallet. "Now we will have to find something for your sister."

We look in many shops until we find a black sweater with a beaded collar. It will look beautiful on Sally with her long hair.

"That was fun," Obaachan says. "I was poor for so long that I've never gotten used to money. I forget to spend it. I regret not buying more things for your mother when she was a child."

"Did she want a lot of things?"

"I thought so, then. Here. Let's throw a coin in the river like your father does." We walk the short block to the river. Obaachan hands me a nickel.

"Dad believes in luck." I throw my coin, wishing that time could stop and everything stay the same.

"May you shine at your new school, and your shyness float away from you like a leaf on a stream." Obaachan tosses hers high into the air, then watches it flip into the water. "I will not always be here," she says.

Metaphors

The first day of school, Mom drops me off on her way to volunteering at the Al Gore headquarters. She peers up at the big building on the hill, with its pillars and statues. "Don't be scared."

I gulp. "Maybe I should just go back to my old school."

"This is free because of your hard work."

"Work isn't really hard," I say, which is true. I've seen students sweating, rubbing their eyes, scratching their heads over math equations that seem as easy to me as brushing your teeth. It makes me feel guilty.

"It's half an hour before school starts. Will you be okay?"

"No."

"I promised I'd bring breakfast to our meeting and I want to get my points in about the canvassing strategy."

"George Bush is going to win," I say, because I'm angry at getting left here.

"Don't say such a thing!"

"It's just a feeling." But I know it's true. George Bush will win; it makes my stomach hurt.

"Well, change that feeling. Out." She reaches across me and opens the passenger door. Nothing gets to her more than those two words: *George Bush.* "Have a good day. I am very proud of you."

I wave until her car disappears, my stomach in my throat, my breath stuck in my chest.

Unlike the public school, which was in one brick building with a cement play area, my new school is in many buildings scattered across a park with rolling hills.

I wish that Sally could come here, too. She would be so excited by the two old mansions that house classrooms and the smaller buildings that fit right in with the trees. If Sally were here, I would feel safe and comfortable, even though it is my first day.

I find a bench and try to meditate, using the new mantra Obaachan has given me: *Om Mani Padme Hum.* I keep my eyes open so I don't look weird.

A cardinal flies onto the bench across from me and we watch each other. Its red wings puff out; its tiny head tilts. *See my peace,* the cardinal seems to say. *I know my place in the world. I* am watching so carefully I almost feel I *am* the bird, the way years ago, I was the spider. Then the bell rings. My heart stops. I move slowly toward the building.

At the public school, I had about twenty-six kids in my class. Here, there're only thirteen kids in the whole fifth grade.

First period is poetry. The teacher's name is Karen; she never says her last name. Poetry is about the senses, she tells us, and metaphor, which relates unlike things in ways that make sense. It reminds me a little of koans.

We spend the class creating metaphors. Anger is a red sword. The mind is a shooting arrow. Memory is a kaleido-scope.

Second period is botany, where we examine leaves under a microscope and walk through the grounds of the school iden-tifying plants.

The only problem I have is that no one knows that I'm invisible. So a girl compliments me on my pink coat. A boy asks me for directions to the greenhouse. In history, when Mr. Kraus calls on me, he expects me to answer. "Do you need me to repeat the question?" He walks up to my desk. "Why do we call America the melting pot?"

He has a kind face, with round, owlish glasses. I'd like to please him, but my voice is stuck.

"Why the melting pot?" His eyes are laser beams. Hands go up all around, but he sticks to me like a dentist to your mouth.

I picture a ship coming in to Ellis Island, the scared, poor people stepping off, not speaking English, hoping to start a new life, willing even to change their names. They are immigrants like my mom and like my dad's parents. They climb a ladder and dive into a giant pot, offer themselves as ingredients, then dissolve into nothing. "Different races and religions came to this country for a better life," I whisper.

"Louder, please."

"Their ethnicity was lost as they tried to be American."

"Not always lost," Mr. Kraus says. "Sometimes muted."

My face gets hot. I didn't answer correctly. I sounded lame.

"The phrase actually came from a play by a Jewish immigrant. The play has now been forgotten, but the phrase lives on. And that is an interesting point about ethnicity, Lin. There was the need to assimilate, and there was resistance to assimilate."

After class, he stops me. "Voice is power. We all need that kind of power."

"Yes, sir."

I look forward to orchestra and seeing Ms. Nga, the one person I know at this school. But she isn't in the orchestra room. I hesitate at the door, then make my way to the front so there'll be room for my cello. I hear whispers. "Ms. Nga is getting married."

She told me last lesson that she was engaged, but hearing

it again makes me feel sad inside, like the time I saw the Strausses' orange cat lying in the street, unmoving.

The whispers grow into loud talking. Five minutes pass. A couple of students put their instruments back in their cases.

Finally, Ms. Nga comes in. She holds her finger up to her mouth and gives a fierce look at the students, who grow silent, immediately.

She passes out sheet music. The students lift their instruments, and we begin to play a simple piece, *Musette*, by Bach. Metaphor: the orchestra is an old man limping through a street.

I play lazily along with everyone else and focus on getting home to Obaachan.

In the middle of the song, Ms. Nga sets down her baton hard. If I didn't know her, I would be scared, like my first day with Sister April, who ended up being nice. "You play as if you're watching TV!" She stares into her space, her mouth hanging open, her hand mechanically playing an invisible violin. "Where is the feeling?" Her eyes dart to me. "Lin. Come here."

I think, *She noticed my laziness; now I will be in trouble.*

"Bring your cello."

I pick up my cello. She grabs a chair and sets it facing the class. "Play Bach's Suite number 2. With *feeling*."

I can feel all the eyes on me. My mouth goes dry. Anger makes my heart pound. This is my first day and Ms. Nga is calling attention to me! Doesn't she know me?

I focus my eyes on the floor and say my mantra.

"Go ahead."

I always dread that first note, but then I get caught up in the music, so I'm sorry when the song comes to a finish.

I look up. The class is applauding, smiling, nodding their heads at me, and I am permanently visible.

After school, I watch the kids pair up or become groups. I'm used to walking or taking the bus with Sally, but she gets out a half hour earlier than me.

"Hey." I hear a voice behind me. "Cello girl! Wait up."

I stop. Behind me, a girl is rushing. "Hi! Remember me?"

I don't.

"Violin." She holds up her case.

I nod.

"Keisha King."

"Lin O'Neil," I manage.

"That cello is almost as big as you are," she says. "Your playing is wicked amazing."

I smile to thank her.

"Which way is your house?"

I point.

"I go that way, too. Wanna walk together?"

"Okay."

"What street?"

"Angell Street," I whisper.

"I'm on Hope. Isn't that something? Hope and Angel? Angels give hope. We sure hope there are angels." Keisha walks with a bouncy step, swinging her violin case back and forth. "What do you think of Ms. Nga? She came last year to shape up the orchestra. But she is so strict. Did you notice that boy playing the timpani? Is he cute, or what? Did you find a boy you like yet? I try to pick one the first day. It makes the year more interesting. Not that I ever get together with the boy. I have relatives in this cemetery. I like to say hello to them when I pass. See that sculpture on top of that headstone. My brother made that and stuck it on top. It gets taken down, then he puts it back up. He thinks he's an artist. My dad is from Providence and his dad, too. My mom's from Louisiana. She hates it here. Do you have relatives in that graveyard?"

"No."

"My mom says that if you meet someone, they'll know people you know within six people. Anywhere in the world."

I nod my head.

"Am I bugging you?"

I am so horrified that my voice comes out loudly. "No! It's just I'm shy."

"Don't sweat it. There's tons of shy people at that school, in case you haven't noticed. That's why they're there. We're a regular nerd herd. I've been here since third grade."

"Do you like it?"

"Are you kidding? I love it. My school before was all about discipline. My teacher there would stand on his desk and yell at us through a megaphone. Do you like it?"

"Yes. Very much. I wish my sister could come here."

"Why can't she come? Her grades not good enough?"

"Maybe not."

"My brother doesn't go here, either. He's only good at art. I'm on scholarship, but don't tell anyone. Some kids kind of look down at you if you are."

"Me, too," I admit.

"Cool. You know how much tuition is to that place?"

"No." It never occurred to me to wonder.

"Twenty thousand dollars a year."

"Wow!"

"Yeah. Look, there's Amelia, Erika, and Hannah. They are so stuck-up. They're always together. Strength in numbers, my dad always says. Now there're two of us; that's a number. We can sit together at lunch."

"Okay."

"Want to come over to my house? My mom's home today, so I can have friends over."

It's the first invitation to someone's house I've ever had, but I think of Obaachan waiting with a snack all prepared. "Maybe another day."

"Okay. This is where I turn. Want me to show you where I live? That way you can just come over, whenever."

"Okay."

As we turn onto Hope Street, I see a police cruiser parked in front of a two-story yellow house. "Who lives there?" My heart beats fast, because I know the answer: Matt Perino.

"I don't know their name. There's a policeman, a mom, a grandma, and three boys: two in high school, one about our age. We moved here a couple of years ago from the west side, but I still don't know that many people. Here's my house."

Keisha's house is a two-family like ours.

"Weird-looking, isn't it?" Keisha says.

"I like purple."

"You sure you won't come in?"

"My grandmother will be waiting for me."

"Well, see you tomorrow."

"Bye."

If I weren't in middle school, I would skip home; I'm so happy to have a friend, especially one who talks so much. That makes things easy.

I cross the street on my way back, walking past Matt's house, noticing the basketballs, baseball mitts, and a couple of skateboards in the yard. As I reach the corner, I see Sally, Molly, and Heather hanging out in front of the minimart. All of them, even Sally, are smoking.

Sowing Seeds

ome here." Sally shakes me awake. "You won't believe this."

"What time is it?"

"It's only nine-thirty; you're like an old lady, falling asleep at nine. It's the homework from your new glamorous school; it's sucking the life out of you."

I follow her into the living room. "It's cold."

"Why didn't you put your slippers on?"

"I'm asleep."

"You *were* asleep. Shhhh." She motions to my parents' room, where the news is playing on their TV. "Six months later and they're still waiting for the election to be overturned and Gore to be *crowned*."

"Presidents aren't crowned."

"Shhh." She points at Obaachan's room. "Ears like a coyote's." Sally sits down at the computer. I shove next to her on the chair. "Look at this site I just found. You won't believe it."

On the screen are photographs of men. She clicks on a photograph, and a story comes up telling what the men like to do, eat, what sports they play, what religion they are.

"It's a menu of men. If you want a boyfriend, you just pick one from the menu, write to them, and arrange a date. It's limitless." Sally clicks on man after man. The photos all look like they were taken on vacation: the men in baseball caps or basketball uniforms or holding a fishing rod.

"Why do they all say they like to work out," I complain. "That's so boring."

"It means they're really buff."

"Have you written to anyone?"

"You have to be eighteen and have a credit card. I'm thinking of *borrowing* Mom's, but then if she gets the bill and finds out, she'll flip her lid."

"I thought you liked Walker Briggs?"

"He moved away years ago. I liked Hamden Clark, but then he puked at the school assembly and it was just *so* unattractive. Boys my age are just . . . uncouth. That's what Heather and I decided, so we're only going out with older men."

"Sally," Dad calls from the room. "Are you still up?"

Sally clicks the X in the corner. The menu of men disappears. "I'm just finishing my paper." We tiptoe back into our room. "Night, Mom. Night, Dad."

"Night, honey," Dad says.

"Don't wake your sister," Mom adds.

"Okay," she replies, which makes me giggle.

Once in our room, Sally lights a cigarette. She swats at the smoke. I can't believe that my parents don't smell it. Maybe they just can't imagine one of their children smoking.

I know that I should tell on her, but then what would happen? She'd probably never speak to me again.

"Guess what?" she says.

"What?"

"Heather is already doing it."

"Doing what?"

That cracks her up. She practically chokes on her smoke. "It! With a boy whose dad owns a Cumberland Farms. They go in the back of the store where the cases of sodas and boxes of chips are stacked."

I was in the back room of a Cumby's once, when Dad stopped for gas and I had to use the restroom. It was dark, and a liquid was on the floor. I wasn't sure if it was water or something worse. "I don't think that's such a good thing."

"It is if you're careful."

"Are you *doing it?*"

"Nah. Not yet."

"Cigarettes give you wrinkles and bad breath."

"I choose my own path."

"You do?" It seems to me she tries to be like everybody else.

"Always have. Always will."

"Are you really going to write to boys on the computer?"

"As soon as I figure out how."

"It seems dangerous."

"What do you know? You don't care about boys."

I don't correct her. I haven't even told Keisha that there is one boy I do care about, although I've never really figured out why. I haven't told her that when I walk by his house, I feel happy, just because he's there.

"Go to bed, kiddo. And when you wake up at some ungodly hour, be quiet, okay? Your feet make cracking noises."

"They do not."

I sleep fitfully, the way I do before a big test. When I wake up, it is only four-thirty. I grab the flashlight and my diary and begin to write down my dreams first thing, like Obaachan taught me, trying to keep my pencil from scratching on the paper and waking Sally.

In the first dream, Sally was in a smoky room surrounded by boys. Each time I tried to get near her, the smoke got thicker until she disappeared. In the second, Ms. Nga was a cherry tree in full bloom. Her fiancé came along and began to blow a tremendous wind at her. She waved her branches to try and fend him off, but it didn't help. In a few seconds, all of her blossoms were gone.

I've seen her fiancé now, twice, when he came to our school. He sat scowling in the back of the classroom while we played. He had a way of squinting that reminded me of President Bush, like he was so used to telling lies, there wasn't any truth left in him.

I hear the kettle whistle a second, then stop. I put on my slippers and tiptoe into the kitchen. Obaachan is pouring tea into two cups. "Ah, there you are," she says.

"Did you hear me up?"

"There is so much snow that the world seems completely still. Quiet can wake you up as surely as noise."

"I like the snow."

She peers at me. "We're worried this morning?"

"I don't know." If I tell her about Sally, I am tattling. Besides, how can I mention smoking and "doing it" and men on the computer. "I dreamed about Ms. Nga."

"A very fine person, your Ms. Nga."

I sit down and sip my tea. "Sometimes I see things . . . in my mind and . . ." I don't know how to explain.

"It seems like too much?"

"Yes. Like Ms. Nga. I dream that bad things are happening to her, and when I see her, I feel sad. She's getting married, but every time she talks about her fiancé, my stomach hurts. And there are other things I see, too."

"I'll tell you a secret."

"What?"

"This . . . vision . . . it can be turned off."

"Turned off?"

"Like water."

"How?"

"You decide."

"But then . . . will it be turned back on?"

"You can also decide that. It is all in your power."

"Oh."

"In Tokyo, after a while, I quit the factory and began making clothes. Often, while I was measuring or fitting a dress, the customer would talk to me about her life. She might ask for advice and I would give it to her. Soon, more people began to call on me for advice than for sewing. I became known as *Senkakusha*, a seer. Some of the women were desperate and called on me many times. It started to make me tired. So, I turned off that flow of thought, and I just focused on fitting and sewing, and I was less tired."

"Did you keep it turned off?"

"Eventually I learned how to measure it out so that I didn't give every piece of my energy away."

"But what about Ms. Nga?"

"Remember when I first met you; I gave you a lotus seed?"

"I still have it."

"Lotus blossoms are very special. They are a symbol of purity, because out of a dirty pond, they flower. That is why the word *lotus* is in the mantra I taught you."

"*Om Mani Padme Hum?*"

"Yes. *Padme* means 'lotus.' Just as the lotus grows out of the mud, so our mind can grow out of the mud of our self-centeredness and desire, and be enlightened."

"Yes."

"Someday, do me a favor."

"Of course."

"Plant that seed."

"Will it still be good?"

"That is the other miraculous thing about the lotus. The seeds can last up to five hundred years."

"I'll plant it."

"I am very sorry about Ms. Nga. It will be sad if her husband is not a good man like your father."

"Is there anything I can do? I mean, what is the point of knowing things if there's nothing I can do to help?"

"I have often asked myself that very question." Obaachan sighs. "Maybe *you* can plant some kind of seed in her . . . a seed of doubt?"

"I'll try." It seems impossible, although that is what I do when I tell Sally that smoking will make her sick, smelly, and wrinkly.

❧

At school on Monday, I tell Keisha to go on without me and I find Ms. Nga in the music room.

"Ah, Lin. You must be psychic," Ms. Nga says. "I was just thinking of you. The Junior Philharmonic is having auditions next week. I called your mom this morning. She said it was okay if you want to try out."

"Is Keisha auditioning?"

"No. I'm afraid not. You are the only student here who I suggested. You and Keisha have become friends? That's so nice."

"Yes, she's fun."

"So will you? I know it's scary, but you mustn't let fear get in the way of your life. I'm hearing such good things about you here at school. You're doing well."

"I'll audition."

"Great."

"Ms. Nga?"

"Yes."

"I was wondering about your fiancé, Mr. Kim? Is he Vietnamese, too?"

"No. He's Korean. Isn't it funny: Korean, Vietnamese, Chinese, Japanese, Thai . . . all such different cultures. Yet, some people look at us and think Asians are all the same, which is like saying the French are the same as the Germans. My parents wanted me to marry Vietnamese, but now they accept him. I guess they figure a Korean husband is better than no husband."

"When are you getting married?"

"This summer. I will invite you and your family."

I try to look pleased. "That would be nice."

Ms. Nga puts her jacket on.

"Ms. Nga?"

"Yes, Lin?"

"Is Mr. Kim . . . nice?"

"He can be nice." She frowns. "He's not always so easy to please. Sometimes, he is in a very bad mood."

"Oh."

"I guess *nice* is not a word I imagine when I think of him. *Serious*, maybe. *A little stern*. He thinks I am very frivolous, which he disapproves of. Perhaps he'll be happier after the wedding."

"Will *you* be happier after the wedding?" I look at the floor.

"What a question!" She laughs. "I'm thirty-six. My parents are embarrassed that I am still unmarried."

"But they must be proud that you have a good job and perform in the symphony and have friends."

"My friends and I have fun together. And I do have . . . freedom."

"I guess that changes after you get married."

"Maybe." She picks up her briefcase. "Goodness, I think that's the most you've ever spoken to me at once. Such interest in marriage. Don't worry. You have plenty of time for that. Do you need a ride home?"

"No, thank you." I bow to her, hoping that my seed will sprout, grow tendrils, and blossom into doubt.

Charades

In New England, spring begins in May. It isn't until then that I accept Keisha's invitation to go over to her house. Our friendship so far has consisted of me walking her home, something that allows me to pass Matt Perino's house twice in one day. Now that the weather is warm, he's out with his brothers playing basketball or tossing a baseball on the front lawn. When we walk by, I try not to look at him. I wonder what it is about him that has always made me feel funny.

"That boy who plays the viola," Keisha is saying. "I asked him what he wanted to do when he grows up and you know what he said?"

"No."

"Cats."

"Cats?" I giggle.

"And I'm like, the *musical*? 'No,' he goes, 'feline behavior. I want to be an animal psychologist.' Do you think that's weird? I mean . . . What? He's going to do kitty analysis?" Keisha tries her front door. Then she looks under a potted plant. "Nathan always does this. He locks the door and hides the key. Once, I had to climb in through the window!" She pounds on the door.

Finally, it cracks open. Nathan is tall and looks about Sally's age. "No soliciting." He tries to close the door, but Keisha is fast. She wedges herself in the opening, then slides in.

Another boy stands watching. "Today's entertainment," he says.

"I have a friend here," Keisha says, scolding her brother. "So act like a human being, for once."

"Hi, Keisha," the other boy says.

"What's going on?" Keisha's mom appears from the kitchen, a dish towel in her hand. "Oh, is this Lin?" She has a pretty southern accent. "So glad to finally meet you. Come on in and have a snack."

"Hi, Keisha," the boy repeats.

Keisha doesn't answer. We follow her mom into the kitchen. "Who's that boy?" I whisper.

"That's Gregory, Nathan's friend. They're stuck together like glue."

"I think he likes you."

"Yeah, he does, but that's because I won't give him the

time-o-day. If I did, he wouldn't be interested anymore. That's the first rule of thumb with boys; never let them know you're interested."

"Cookies and milk?" Keisha's mom sets a plate in front of us.

"Thank you, Mrs. King." I have a pang of missing Obaachan, although she's the one who told me I should go to Keisha's house. As Sally would put it, *Get a life*.

"Those have peanuts in them, in case you're allergic, but the others don't. They just have coconut."

"They're very good. Thank you."

"You're so polite."

Nathan and Gregory skulk in. They each grab a handful of cookies.

Mrs. King swats at them with the dish towel. "Put those back. You would think you were raised in a barn. One cookie at a time." She pushes the plate away from the boys. "I am gonna water my plants and I better not hear any scrapping between you two."

"We'll play nice as angels." Nathan puts his hands into a prayer position.

The boys flop down at the table. "I know you." Gregory points to me. "My dad owns Café Soiree on Benefit Street. You're always walking down by the river with that old lady who looks like she's from another planet."

"That's my grandmother."

"How rude," Keisha scolds.

"A nice planet," Gregory corrects.

"Y'all want to play something," Nathan says.

"Don't say y'all," Keisha says. "It makes you sound like a hick."

"We're from the South," Nathan argues, "even if you forget. Yankee prep school snob."

"Shut up."

"What do you want to play?" I ask, to keep the peace.

"How about Spin the Bottle?" Gregory suggests.

Nathan shoves him. "I'm not gonna kiss my *sister*!"

"You can kiss *her*." Gregory points to me. "If it lands on Keisha, kiss *her* instead."

"Her name is Lin," Keisha says.

"You just want to kiss Keisha," Nathan taunts.

"Shut up!" The two boys wrestle each other to the floor.

"Neither of us is kissing either of you." Keisha makes a gesture like she's swatting them away.

"Hey, that's it," Nathan says. "We'll play charades."

Keisha clears the plates and puts them in the dishwasher. "We'all don't want to be with you'all."

"Come on," Nathan begs. "I'll let you play my SimCity later. Greg and I are boring each other stiff."

"For how long?" Keisha offers.

"Half an hour."

"An hour."

"All right."

We follow them through a hall. Every wall is filled with artwork, paintings that don't look like anything I've ever seen. In the living room, a large sculpture hangs in front of the window. It is made of all kinds of materials.

"Where'd that mobile come from?" Keisha says. "It looks like it's from another planet."

"It *is* another planet," Nathan explains. "It's a sculpture of the solar system. I just finished it."

"That doesn't look like any solar system I've ever seen," Gregory says.

"It's an abstract representation."

"What's it made out of?" I ask.

"That pear shape is made of foil and toilet paper rolls. That's supposed to be Mars. Saturn is made of an orange stuck with cloves. Earth is trash. The bottle caps represent shooting stars. The fabric scraps are UFOs and stuff like that. The Super Glue is supposed to be invisible, but it's made a nasty sheen on the twigs."

"There's twelve extra planets there," Keisha says.

"Thanks. I think it's magnificent, too."

"Enough with the art appreciation," Greg says. "Let's play."

"We need ground rules," Nathan says.

"Girls against boys," Keisha says. "Who's first?"

"Let's do just TV shows and movies," Gregory says. "I don't like doing people or places because someone always chooses a person or place I don't know."

"That makes sense," Keisha says. *"Not."*

"A *place*," Gregory explains, "like Taj Mahal. Or a person, like Einstein."

"Who doesn't know Taj Mahal or Einstein?" Keisha argues.

"How about Spokane, Washington?" Gregory says. "Would you guess Spokane? I used to live there. People drive around with rifles and dead deer strapped to their cars."

"Whatever," Keisha says. "Movies and TV shows."

The idea of performing a charade in front of these two boys makes my face hot, but I guess it's better than kissing. Plus, I am worried that I won't be able to guess any because I don't watch TV or movies much. "Can we do books?"

"Girls read different books than boys," Nathan says. "How about Web sites?"

"No way," Keisha says. "The only one we would all know is My Space and Google."

"Okay. I'll go first." Gregory holds up his fingers.

"Two words," Nathan says.

Gregory jumps around the room like a monkey, dragging his arms on the ground.

"Ape," Nathan says. *"Planet of the Apes."*

"That's not two words," Keisha says.

A movie I've never seen pops into my head. *"King Kong."*

"Yes!" Gregory says.

"You should have connected it with our last name," Nathan says.

"It's our turn," Keisha says. "Lin guessed, so she goes."

I feel my face get red. "You can go for me, Keisha?"

"No," Nathan says. "That's not the rules."

"I've never played before," I fib; I have played with Sally and Dad.

"You did pretty well guessing," Greg argues.

"I'll go for her," Keisha says. "It's girls against boys, so we can decide who goes. Until she gets the hang of it." Keisha holds up two fingers, then she curls her body up like someone who's scared.

"Hide," Nathan says.

"Ball," Gregory says.

She shakes her head.

"Duck?" Nathan asks.

She makes the "sounds like" signal.

Again, the answer pops into my mind. *"Tuck Everlasting."*

"Yes!" Keisha jumps up. "Two for us!"

The boys stare at me. "How did you get that?"

"I read that book."

"We said no books," Nathan argues.

"It's a movie, too," Keisha says.

"I never heard of it," Gregory adds.

"The author lives in Providence," I say.

"Did you figure these out in advance?" Gregory accuses.

"Duh!" Keisha says. "Nathan came up with the game two seconds ago. Nathan went first. Lin's just good at it. She's practically a genius, anyway."

"Right," Nathan says. "And me and Gregory are Alfred Einstein."

"Albert," Keisha corrects.

"Okay. I've got one!" Gregory says. "Can I go?"

"Whatever," Keisha says.

Gregory holds up four fingers.

"Four words!"

He starts scrubbing the floor.

"Wash. Scrub. Maid," Keisha says.

He scrubs more and more wildly. We are laughing so much, it's hard for anyone to speak.

"Lunatic," Nathan says. "Lunatic asylum. Crazy maid."

Gregory points to his hand. *Sponge*, I think. *SpongeBob SquarePants*. Sally used to watch it. But this time, I don't say anything; I don't want them to think I'm weird.

"Washcloth," Keisha says.

"Wax! Sponge!" Nathan says. Gregory nods emphatically, then draws a square in the air.

"*SpongeBob SquarePants*," Nathan shouts.

"Yes! Victory for the boys' team." Gregory does a dance.

"Excuse me." Keisha is all attitude. It's funny, because at school, she's almost as quiet as me. "*SpongeBob SquarePants*? Exactly how is that four words?"

"*Sponge. Bob. Square. Pants*." Gregory counts on his hand. "Four words."

"It's two words. *SpongeBob* is one word. *SquarePants* is another. Disqualification for the boys' team."

"It is not," Nathan says. "It's four words. Get the TV guide."

Keisha rushes out and returns with the TV guide, a look of triumph on her face. She shows them.

"Moron!" Nathan whacks Gregory on the head.

"Hey," Gregory defends. "My aunt gave me an I.Q. test and I scored in the top ten percentile, so who's the moron?"

"Do you know what I.Q. stands for?" Nathan retorts. "Idiot queer."

They begin wrestling. Keisha again does her yawn. "Idyllic quandary," she says. "Interest-free quantity. Ivory Queen. Illustrious Quest. Ironic quack. Infinite quality." Both boys stop and look up at her with interest.

"I'll bet your I.Q. is way up there, Keisha," Gregory says. "Why don't you come over to my house and my aunt can give you the test."

"Talk to the hand."

"What is the sound of one hand clapping?" Nathan holds up a hand, then he flicks his fingers down to make a snapping noise. "The world according to Bart Simpson."

I look at the clock. I've been here two hours, the first after-school hours I've ever been away from Obaachan. A wave of homesickness hits me. Out the window, the sky is gray and dusky. By contrast, Nathan's solar system looks like a colorful patchwork quilt. "It's going to fall." The words come out of my mouth before I can stop them.

They all follow my eyes to Nathan's art, which is hanging perfectly still and in one piece.

"Huh?"

"Nothing," I say quickly.

"What should we do now?" Gregory says.

But no one answers, because a moment later, there's a cracking sound; the twig holding the planets snaps, and the pieces of Nathan's mobile crash to the floor.

"Hell." Nathan rushes over and collects the pieces.

"How did you know that was going to fall?" Gregory turns to me.

I shrug.

"Freaky."

"I'd better go," I say. "My grandmother's waiting for me."

I walk home feeling like, for an afternoon, I got to masquerade as Sally, like in a story we read in class, where two friends switch places in each other's life.

As I pass Matt's house, the door opens and he appears like magic. "Hi, Lin." He picks a newspaper up off the lawn.

"Hi, Matt," I finally manage.

"You remember me, don't you?"

"Yes."

"I'm surprised."

"We were in kindergarten together."

"Right. You always won at being the stillest."

"And catechism with Sister April."

"Did you know that Sister April quit being a nun?"

"No."

"She got married and now she works as a nurse. She's friends with my mom." He points to my uniform. "You're at 'the hill' now with the smart kids."

"Yeah. I changed schools."

"You're the one person I've seen who looks good in that uniform."

I feel myself blush. "Thanks."

"I mean *brown*. That's gotta be the worst color to have to wear every day."

"Yeah. Well, I . . . It's getting dark. I'd better . . ."

"You'd better get home before it's dark."

"Yeah."

"I'll see you around."

The whole walk home, I go over the brief exchange. *Hi, Lin.* That means that all the times I've passed his house, he's known who I was. He's remembered *me*. *You're the one person I've seen who looks good in that uniform.* That was a compliment. *I'll see you around.* Does that mean we'll be friends?

I can't wait to tell Obaachan all of my news. Even the falling mobile. Why do I know things sometimes before they happen? "Obaachan." I rush in the front door. "I'm back."

"In here," Mom calls from Obaachan's room. The windows are open. Mom is changing the sheets. "You're late. I was worried."

"I stopped at Keisha's. Didn't you get my message?"

"Your message said you'd be home at five. It's now five-thirty. And where's your sister? She should've been home two hours ago and she never called. I need to talk to her right away. Is this what goes on when I'm at work, expecting you to behave responsibly?"

"Where's Obaachan?"

"At the hospital. Just a few days of tests. Don't worry." She sighs and sits on the bed. "I'm sorry. I'm just a little tense. It's not your fault. It's about Sally."

"What kind of tests?"

Mom forces a smile. "On her blood. Don't worry. This is an illness she's carried a long time. She'll be home soon. What a day; everything going wrong at once, and I can't reach your dad to save my life."

"What about Sally?"

"Mrs. Caros called. She was driving past the school and saw Sally with a gang of kids. Sally was smoking. Did you know this? Lin, did you know she smokes?"

I don't answer because I don't care right now whether Sally smokes. Obaachan is in the hospital and Mom is acting like she went to get her hair done. *"When* will Obaachan be back? How long will she be in the hospital?"

Maybe if I'd have come home right after school, she would still be here.

Lines

The rope that divided Sally's room into two has long disappeared, but you can still tell there's a line down the middle. My half of the room is tidy, my bed made, my clothes put away. On my bed is the heart pillow Mom gave me on Valentine's Day, my Build-A-Bear in her pink dress, and the stuffed green snake Dad won for me at the fair. My books are neatly arranged by series: *Betsy, Tacy, and Tib; Little House on the Prairie; American Girls*. Above my bed is a poster of Yo-Yo Ma and a Hello Kitty calendar.

On the floor of Sally's side is a growing pile of clothes, her Walkman, notebooks, CDs, old copies of *Teen* and *Seventeen* magazines, overdue library books, and whatever fast food wrappers she's forgotten to hide from Mom. Her bed is never made. Taped to the wall are her drawings of celebrities: Madonna and Mariah Carey. She tore down her *Spice Girls* poster after they broke up.

Dad refers to our room as *A Tale of Two Cities* (the "best of times" is my side; the "worst of times" is Sally's side), or as "split screen."

Sally isn't amused by either name.

After Obaachan is moved to a hospital in Boston, though, my side starts to resemble Sally's. I put off my homework until the last minute and get my first B's, jeopardizing my scholarship. I miss so many rehearsals at the Junior Philharmonic that I am put on probation. I even see less of Keisha, who complains that she is now stuck with Gregory and Nathan. I stop meditating and going to church. I stay up late, watching TV with Sally: *Friends*, *3rd Rock from the Sun*, and *Boy Meets World*.

On the first Saturday of summer, when I get to the breakfast table, Mom, Sally, and Dad look at *me* like I'm from another planet.

Mom points to the clock. "Every day, you get up five minutes later than the day before."

"She looks hungover," Sally says.

"How do you know about that?" Dad glares at her.

Sally shrugs. "TV."

"Maybe you watch too much TV." He has not gotten over her smoking.

"Look what I made for breakfast for you?" Mom pushes a plate toward me. *"Tamago."*

"Thank you." I force a piece into my mouth. It tastes nothing like Obaachan's.

"Don't I get a special meal?" Sally says.

Dad plops a sugar doughnut on her plate.

"Speaking of doughnuts," Sally says. "There's a concert at Boston Common."

"How is that speaking of doughnuts?" Mom says.

"It's an all-girl band, a fund-raiser to promote racial harmony."

"Racial harmony?" Dad jokes. "They should come and visit the O'Neil house."

"If we went to Boston, we could visit Obaachan at the hospital," I say. Since she moved to Boston two weeks ago, we have only been once. She was so sick, she couldn't speak to us.

"How much are the tickets?" Dad asks.

"Only fifty dollars, and it's for a good cause."

"Fifty dollars! For each of us? That's two hundred dollars."

"Well, I wasn't going to go with *you*, exactly."

"Then with who?"

"Heather and Courtney and Allison, if she can pull her face away from the mirror long enough to do anything. Her dad has a Mercedes. He can drive us. It will be so cool to drive up in a Mercedes."

"What happened to Molly?" Dad says.

"Oh, I am so done with Molly, Dad. Where have you been?"

"I don't know where I've been. Probably working overtime to buy clothes at Limited Too."

"I am so over Limited Too."

"What is this insertion of 'so' into every sentence?" Mom reprimands. "Speak English."

"I'm speaking *American*. You are so out of it, Mom."

"At least you used the word properly in that sentence."

"*So*, do I get to go?"

"No concert," Mom and Dad say at once.

"Don't you hate it when they do that?" She turns to me. "They might as well be Siamese twins. One body. Two heads."

"You're still on restriction for smoking."

"It's been, like, weeks!"

"I knew a boy whose dad put him on restriction for a whole year," I say. Actually, Keisha knew the boy. "He was working at his dad's factory and threw a match into a garbage pail. The whole place burned down."

"Gee, thanks." Sally picks up a felt pen and doodles a girl with a guitar.

"Why can't we visit Obaachan today?"

"That's all she thinks about," Sally says.

Dad and Mom look at each other. "I don't think there are visiting hours today," Mom says. "They're low on staff."

"So?" My voice sounds angry.

"You sound like your sister with that tone," Mom scolds.

"So?" Sally says. "What's wrong with sounding like me?"

We both fold our arms.

"A teen and a preteen," Mom says. "I must've won the lottery."

"I've got an idea," Dad offers. "It's a beautiful day. What do you say we go fishing?"

"Instead of a concert! No way." Sally storms off.

"Come on, Linny. Go fishing with me. You can't just stay inside all the time and mope."

"I don't feel like it." I look down so I won't have to see my dad's disappointment. On the table is the newspaper. The headline says: "Missing Boy." The boy grins from the photograph. Something about his face reminds me of Cole at my old school, the boy everyone made fun of.

Mom says, "There's sandwiches you two can take."

"Uh-huh." I stare at the boy.

"Did she say yes?" Dad asks.

"I think so," Mom says.

"Huh?" I look up.

"You just agreed to go to the beach."

"I did?"

"Come on, kiddo. We're a family. We do things together."

"Okay." It's hard to say no to my dad. "But I want to visit Obaachan soon."

Dad goes to get his fishing gear. I unfold the paper and read the story: Vincent Serrins, a nine-year-old, disappeared from his front yard two days ago. One person saw him get into a blue van. Another saw him walking down Waterman Street. There have been kidnappings in Florida and California this year, the paper points out, but not in Rhode Island.

Mom clears the table. "Sally drew on my tablecloth."

"Don't wash it," I say. "It's a good drawing."

"Ready?" Dad grabs the newspaper. "Do you want to bring a book?"

"No." I follow Dad out to his truck. "Can I stop at the church? I just want to run in for a second."

"Sure." He drives the few blocks to our church. "Take your time." He opens the newspaper.

The church is almost empty. I dip my fingers in holy water, make the sign of the cross, then slide into the pew, and kneel. "Kneel O'Neil," Sally used to kid me, when I was little.

I bow my head and say Hail Marys and Our Fathers. I ask God a favor: "Please, bring Obaachan home. Make her well, if you can, but at least bring her home." Then I *sit*. I meditate for the first time since she went into the hospital. The familiar blankness flows into me, the feeling of being everything and nothing at once. But it doesn't last. Instead, an image comes into my mind, sharp as any photograph. It's the boy, Vincent Serrins, hunched up in the corner of a small wooden building. He's alone and scared.

"Okay, kiddo?" Dad says when I climb into his truck.

"Uh-huh."

"Boy! Am I excited. Remember that albacore I caught that time. It was like *The Old Man and the Sea*. Me pulling it. It fighting back. Your mom cooked it with chili and ginger. Best meal I ever had."

I pick up the paper and read the caption under the photograph: "Providence Boy Missing for Two Days."

"What's wrong?"

"Nothing. It's just . . ."

"What?"

"It's hard to say. I keep getting a picture in my mind of where he is."

"Who?" He glances at the paper. "That missing boy?"

"Yeah."

"A feeling?"

"You know. Like when the phone rings and I know who it is."

"That's because it's always Nora," he jokes, then looks serious. "He's been missing for a couple of days. I assumed he was kidnapped and, you know, they'd be finding a body. That's the way it seems to go these days. What a world."

"Yeah. But I think he's alive."

He pulls the truck over. "Tell you what? I have a buddy over at the substation. I did the drywall on his house. How 'bout we stop in and you can tell him what you see. . . . It couldn't hurt."

"The *police* station?"

"The small one. It's right by the Laundromat. We'll just talk privately."

"They'll think I'm a weirdo."

"There are worse things in life than someone thinking you're a weirdo."

When we get to the substation, we're led into a little office and told to wait for the detective. I expect to see a police officer with a uniform and gun, but the man who enters wears blue jeans, a sweatshirt, and a baseball cap. He shakes Dad's hand. "Detective Perino."

My stomach flip-flops.

"Bobby O'Neil. And this is my daughter Lin. I was hoping to talk to Harry Saunders."

"He's retired. Last I heard, he was in Bermuda. Please sit down."

Dad leads me to a chair. "My daughter here has a kind of talent. She has feelings sometimes, about who's calling or what people are going to say."

Matt's dad picks up a paper clip and fidgets with it. "Uh-huh."

Dad holds up the paper. "She was looking at the newspaper, the story about that missing boy . . ."

"Vincent Serrins?"

"Yes, and she got a sort of picture in her mind."

"What kind of picture?" Detective Perino peers at me.

I tug my eyes back to the photo. The clock is ticking. Phones are ringing in the outer office. My mouth is dry.

"Take your time."

I swallow. "I see a shed . . . and he's inside of it."

"A shed?"

"Like a toolshed."

"Is he with anyone?"

"I think he's by himself."

"What else? What's around it?"

Circles and lines, I think, but that seems silly. "I don't know."

He sighs. The paper clip is now straight. He bends it back into shape. "What's he doing in this shed?"

"Rocking. Back and forth like this."

For the first time, he looks right at me, dropping the paper clip. "Vincent Serrins is autistic. He does rock back and forth just like that. Maybe you can draw this place."

"I'm not good at drawing. My sister is."

"Try, Lin," Dad coaxes.

Matt's dad hands me a pad of paper and a pencil. I draw a square for the shed, then lines in front of it. They are parallel and extend far into the distance like any road. I look at my drawing, meditate on it, and then it comes to me. Within the horizontal lines are vertical ones.

"Railroad tracks!" Perino says, grabbing the phone. "Tell dispatch to send search units out along the railroad tracks. The Serrins case. They can comb a ten-mile area radiating from Providence. And not just the tracks in use; all of them."

I close my eyes.

"Is there anything else?"

"No." I feel like I could just slip into a nap.

I hear my dad stand. "My daughter is a private girl. This is just between us."

"You have my word."

My dad gives him his cell phone number. "Please let us know if you find the boy. Come on, Lin."

My legs feel weak as I stand up.

"Thank you so much, young lady. Anytime you have ideas like this, you just come to me."

"We won't tell your mom about this," Dad says as we walk outside. "She might not approve."

"Am I freaky?"

"No! Why would you say that?"

I shrug.

"You come by your . . . talents honestly." He switches to an Irish accent. "My grandmother Mary O'Neil, from County Cork, was a great one for precognition. She predicted the war years before it happened, but it didn't stop her sons from enlisting."

"Did she have red hair like yours?"

"She did, once. It was said her hair turned white overnight when she got the telegram her son Ian had been shot down over Germany. But I imagine that was an exaggeration. At any rate, when I met her, her hair was stark white." He opens the trunk door.

"I've dreamed about her." I hop in.

"Have you?"

"I'm so tired, Dad. I just want to . . . take a nap."

He sighs. "Well, I guess you owe me a fishing trip. I want a rain check. In writing."

"I promise."

"Thanks for going in there today. That took courage."

"But what if I'm wrong about it?"

"What if you're not?"

Stories

Two days after my birthday, on July 6, I get my birthday wish and my prayers answered; Obaachan comes home.

She clings to Mom's arm as she walks in and is so thin I can see her bones, like the skeleton of a frail tree. The treatment has made her lose her hair. "I am never going for *tests* again," she tells Mom. "They kept me in there like it was a jail. No more doctors, Mayumi chan. I mean that."

"I made up your bed," Mom says in a cheery voice. "You must rest and get your strength back."

I take her other arm. I remember when the room was a mystery to me and every object held a secret. Now it is as familiar as when it was mine. I peel back the covers on the bed. "I'll make tea," Mom says.

Obaachan offers me a weak smile. "Lin. I am sorry to be away for so long. You must catch me up on everything. How is Keisha?"

I tell her about Keisha and me taking a swimming class together and about Gregory's family's café, where we sit with Gregory and Nathan and hatch plans that we usually don't carry out. And about my solo with the Junior Philharmonic and my conversation with Matt.

"This boy is special to you?" she asks.

I blush.

"I have missed so much. You are coming into your own."

Then I tell her about me and Dad helping to find the autistic boy, Vincent Serrins.

"So he was there in the shed?"

"In Pawtucket. They took him to the hospital, but he was okay, just dehydrated."

"Ah, it is wonderful when your gift can be used to help others. That is a rare thing."

"Lin!" Mom comes in with tea. "Don't tire her."

"Let her stay. I need to hear what my granddaughter has been up to."

"She hasn't been cleaning her room. I can tell you that. She hasn't been studying like she used to. Five minutes, Lin. No longer." She goes out.

"She's a very bossy lady," Obaachan says.

I hold the tea to her lips. "This will make you feel better."

"I am sorry to be such trouble."

"I'm just glad you're back. Were you lonely at the hospital?" It has been my constant fear.

"It is hard to be lonely at the hospital because they never leave you alone. The nurses come and go at all hours. They should learn that there is such a thing as being too cheerful. I'll tell you . . . when your grandfather Tomo was sick, he wouldn't go to the doctor. Instead, he went to Sensei Ohura, a local wise man. Sensei Ohura told Tomo that one of his ancestors was sitting on his chest and that this was why he had pain. The ancestor was a hungry ghost, one who hadn't made it across to the other side."

"What's a hungry ghost?"

"A ghost who is so attached to this world by desire, they can't cross to the next stage. They are called hungry because their throats are too small to eat or drink."

"That sounds terrible."

"Well, I didn't believe a word of it. I thought Sensei was a kook!" Her voice creaks like old music. "Your grandfather was sick because he smoked too much and drank whiskey. But Sensei gave him herbs and chants and Tomo followed every word of it."

"Did he get better?"

"No, he went blind. This time, Sensei told him that the blindness was because Tomo had witnessed too much suffering. It was a blessing not to see the painful things in the world. Besides, it wasn't true blindness, Sensei told him. True blindness was ignorance and cruelty."

"At least your voice is still in working order." Mom comes in with two cups of miso soup. "You eat, too, Lin."

"Thanks, Mom." I sip the soup.

"I was just telling Lin about your father, Mayumi chan. Once he was blind, he couldn't bear any noise. I could whisper, but he said my voice sounded like screeching monkeys and my footsteps like a herd of elephants."

"Dad never went blind."

"You were gone by then." Obaachan lays her head back and closes her eyes. "What do you know?"

"Nothing, apparently."

"Tomo is waiting for me," Obaachan mumbles. "I only hope his senses are put right. My mother is waiting, too. She will have wondered why I was away so long. . . ."

Mom motions me out. I follow her to the kitchen. "Why isn't she better?"

"She will never be better." A tear rolls down her cheek. "She has been sick a long time."

"Mom."

"Something's in my eye." She covers her face. "I'm sorry. It is all so sad. Her illness. And remembering."

"Remembering what?"

"Childhood. How terrible it was. And stifling."

"What was it like?"

"We lived in a tiny apartment. One room. My parents were always working, although there never seemed to be any money. My father owned a newspaper stand. Grandma sewed clothes. There was cloth everywhere. And straight pins on the floor that I would step on constantly. No one ever talked about anything. I always felt like I was born into the wrong family," she says. "And rice balls."

"Rice balls?"

"Rice balls, oily fish, and pickled cabbage and cucumber. That's what we ate. Occasionally, noodles. Food was completely unimportant to my parents. They could have eaten the same bowl of rice every day for ten years and not cared."

"She's a good cook, now."

"She wasn't then. And the fish. It was scraps: oily and salty."

"So that was what was terrible?"

"Everything was terrible. And them. All they could think about was a war that had happened twenty years earlier. They needed to *get a life*, but they stayed stuck like camels in quicksand."

"Were you sad when you left?"

"No. I was scared, but I was also thrilled. It was like one of those fairy tales: a poor girl stuck in a tiny apartment with her parents who don't approve of her, meets a handsome soldier from the very place she longs to go more than anywhere else in the world. Your father was so kind. He asked me how I felt about this, or what I thought about that. No one had ever done that. When he brought me home to his parents, they were in shock." She laughs. "All of them red haired and blue eyed like him. I was so shy, they didn't know I spoke English. 'What have you done?' His mother pointed at me. 'She's . . . she's . . .' I was horrified to hear those words come out of her mouth. I thought she was going to say: *Japanese*. She finally got the words out. 'She's . . . not Catholic!' Then I surprised everyone. In my best American accent, one I had practiced for years, I said, 'Well, I'll become one of those. Don't you worry!' And his dad bent over with laughter: 'I'll be damned.' Then his mom started laughing, too. And I'll tell you something. I had no idea what Catholic was. Your dad had never mentioned religion. But I wanted to belong. I would be Catholic. I've never regretted it."

"Didn't you miss your parents?" I can't imagine ever being far from my parents or Sally.

"I felt guilty, like I'd escaped from a sinking ship and left them behind. But they wouldn't have come. They would've gone down with the ship."

"Is that why you and Obaachan don't get along?"

"We get along fine." Mom gets up and opens the oven. She pulls out a tin of cupcakes. "These are for your school bake sale. You can frost them once they cool."

"What is wrong with Obaachan? What is her illness?"

"Leukemia. She has had it twenty years. It is a disease from the war, from radiation."

"Is she going to die?"

"Who doesn't die, every moment, changing from one form

to another? What happened to that little baby, Lin, who watched everything and never said a word? Or the girl who studied all the time and didn't have friends? Or the one who was afraid to perform and now plays solos with the Junior Philharmonic? Death is a constant part of life. We just try to pretend it's not there. The unknown! That's what we're all afraid of. Well, I have news for the world. Every second of every day is the unknown."

My mouth drops open. I have never heard my mom speak in such a way. "You sound like Obaachan," I tell her.

"Coming from you, that's a compliment."

People of the Tree

Obaachan told me once about a group of people who worshipped trees. They believed trees had spirits that manifested in the roots and trunk, the leaves and branches. It was a crime to cut a tree, or even to peel bark. The spirits were ancestors. A village equated a small forest.

I think of my body as a tree, a bamboo, light and flexible. I am five feet tall. I weight ninety pounds. My dad can put his hand all the way around both of my wrists and still have room to spare. And I'm flexible. When we do yoga in P.E., I can stretch farther than anyone.

Lately, though, I feel like a log in a river of molasses. My limbs ache. My pants are tight. I can't button my blouses.

"What's wrong with you?" Sally asks me. "You keep dropping things."

We are in our kitchen with Keisha, making a cake for the cake walk at the back-to-school fair. I pick the wooden spoon off the floor and rinse it. "Slippery fingers," I say.

"Isn't that someone who steals?" Keisha says.

"That's sticky fingers," Sally corrects. "Get it. Stuff sticks to your fingers."

It's the first time Sally has hung out with us. Usually, she calls us the fifth-grade babies, or now the sixth-grade babies, since school just started.

"I've got butter fingers." Keisha holds up her hands. "My brother has sculpted with butter. Also, soap, lard, and wax. He's crazy."

"Was that your brother who dropped you off?" Sally asks.

"Yeah."

"I recognize him. He's a sophomore. He hangs out in the art room. Does he have a girlfriend?"

"Who knows?" Keisha shrugs.

I put the kettle on, to make soup for Obaachan, then slump into a chair to wait for it to boil.

"Hey," Sally says. "You're supposed to be helping."

"I don't feel well."

"You don't eat enough junk food. That's your problem."

"Did you hear about Ms. Nga?" Keisha asks.

"Uh-huh."

"What?" Sally says.

"Ms. Nga broke off her engagement," Keisha says. "I wonder what happened. Maybe she fell in love with someone else. Or maybe he cheated on her. Do you know what happened, Lin?"

I shrug, but I do know. Ms. Nga told me about the feeling she got when he came to pick her up, that in going to his car she was "walking off a gangplank."

"Ms. Nga is difficult," Sally says. "She used to hit me with her bow."

I roll my eyes. "She *pretended* she was going to hit Sally with her bow, because Sally was always caterwauling while I was having my lesson, but she never actually hit her."

"Caterwauling?" Sally says. "What the heck is that?"

Keisha chuckles. "That was one of our vocab words this week. It means 'sending out mournful and unnatural sounds.'"

"And the reason she didn't hit me is because I'm fast."

I pour the hot water into the miso paste, then tiptoe to Obaachan's room with the soup. She is sleeping, as she often does these days. In the dim room, the *Enso* painting seems to float, like a circle watching over her.

I leave the soup on the bedside table.

"I wonder if a person can lose so much weight they disappear," Sally is saying, when I come back in.

"What?"

"Obaachan. There's nothing left to her. Here's a fact. Since the Japanese have started eating a Western diet, they've really shot up. It's the hormones in beef."

"That's disgusting," Keisha says. "I'm not eating beef. They found that mad cow disease in Alabama. It turns your brain to sponge. And why? Because they feed vegetarian cows parts of themselves. Me and Lin are studying it in zoology."

"Don't talk about it." Sally holds up her hand. "I eat a Quarter Pounder or a Big Mac just about every day."

"Then how come you're so short?" I ask.

Sally shoots me a look. "Is that sarcasm? Coming from my little sister? Well, I'll be damned. You're turning into a teenager."

A horn honks. "That's Nathan. I'd better go. He hates to wait for even a second. He's such a pain. Why is he always early when I'm having fun, then late when I'm doing something awful, like having detention or taking my violin lesson?" Keisha complains.

Sally rushes to the window. I walk Keisha to the door. "Get some rest, girl," Keisha tells me. "I'm serious. You look bad!"

"Her brother is a major hunk!" Sally says, her eyes glued to the window.

When I wake up in the morning, I am convinced I am dying, or at the very least have appendicitis.

Sally is rushing around the room, shoving books into her backpack, checking her makeup in the vanity mirror. She's never up before I am. "I told Mom you were sick and she said you could sleep in."

"I'll be late for school."

"Once in a lifetime. I don't think it'll kill you. How do you feel?"

"Pain."

"Where pain?"

"Here." My hands go to my belly.

"Pain like a vise that tightens and releases?" Sally asks.

"I think I have appendicitis."

"Mom!" Sally calls.

"What is it?" Mom rushes in. She's wearing her bathrobe. Her hair is in curlers. "Don't scare me."

"Lin's gonna start her period."

My face goes hot.

"No. She's only eleven."

"She was clumsy yesterday and all pale. Besides, I started when I was eleven."

I groan again.

"My little girl growing up? I can't believe it."

"I grew up, too, in case you haven't noticed," Sally says.

"Oh. You! You were grown up when you were three. *In case I haven't noticed.* What do you think I am? Blind?"

I am going to bleed. From *there*. The thought of it makes me shake, gives me chills. I don't want to grow up any more than Mom wants me to.

"Well . . ." Mom places both hands on her head. "I have to get to work. You explain it to her."

"She'd better stay home," Sally says. "You know how sensitive she is."

I'm not thrilled about being discussed like someone's pet, but I don't say anything. Staying home with Obaachan sounds just fine to me.

"Maybe you're right. But school's just started, and I worry she'll miss something."

"She'll catch up. Remember, she's the girl genius! But I'd better stay with her," Sally says dramatically. "This is all going to be very traumatic."

"Obaachan is here."

"Really, this is a sister case. I'm on it."

"Fine. Fine. Just add that to the other twenty days you've missed."

"Ten. Thanks, Mom."

Mom looks at her watch. "My first appointment is in ten minutes. I'd better run." Sometimes I feel like she's rushing away from something rather than to it.

"Good job, Sis. I owe you one." Sally flops on her bed. "Okay, here's the explanation. Once a month you get grouchy for a few days. You feel like your head's going to split open and the slightest thing gets on your nerves. You're clumsy and your brain feels a bit blank. At least that's how I feel. Then you bleed. All that month's eggs drop out of your body or something like that. But you know this stuff. Right?"

"I guess."

"It's not great. But like most things in life, you don't get a choice. I'll get you an aspirin."

"Okay."

The only good thing about the morning is that Obaachan comes out. She is wearing her gray sweatpants and black turtleneck. Her head is wrapped in a scarf. "You girls are home? Is it a holiday?" The happiness in her voice makes me realize how lonely it must be for her now that school has started. All summer, I've had Keisha over here, so that even if Obaachan was resting in her room, she would hear voices.

"Lin doesn't feel well. But don't worry." Sally chuckles. "It's not contagious."

I guide Obaachan to the couch. "Do you want to play cards?"

"Yes. That would be so nice. Sally, will you play with us?"

"No, thanks." Sally's voice is sour, like she's disappointed that she won't have me to herself. "I'll just wait on both of you. You want tea?"

"Yes, please."

"Okay."

I bring out the UNO cards and sit next to Obaachan.

"That bedroom gets old."

"I should open the window in there. It's going to be a nice day."

"I guess every day is nice, when you look at it the right way."

My stomach churns, because I know she means: *when you don't have many days left.*

Sally brings the tea. "Do you feel better, Lin? Has the aspirin kicked in yet?"

"Maybe."

It is so odd to have Sally taking care of us.

"What *is* the matter?" Obaachan frowns.

"Nothing that doesn't happen to any girl," Sally says.

"Sally is making koans," Obaachan jokes.

Sally disappears into the kitchen. Obaachan wins three times in a row. She always wins games. "Shall we work on our Japanese."

"Do you have the energy?"

"Most certainly. It has been too long. Where were we?"

"You were teaching me kanji."

"That's right. We have studied katakana and hiragana. Do you remember?"

"Sort of." Foreign languages and art are my weak subjects. Writing the Japanese characters combines both.

Sally comes in. "Well, if we're having a drawing party, I'll join." She gets her pencil and pad.

"How nice," Obaachan says. "Who knew this day would be so special."

"What's that? Japanese?"

"Uh-huh," I say.

"It looks like Hangman. You know that game? What does it say?"

"Water," Obaachan answers.

Sally copies it perfectly.

"Very good. Sally, you are such an artist."

"I want to be an artist, but there's no money in it. Keisha's brother is an amazing artist. I've seen his work."

There is a pounding on the door. We all three look at it, startled.

"It's me," Mr. Caros booms. "Rico."

Sally gets up and opens the door.

Mr. Caros rushes in, his face and eyes red. "Is your dad here?"

"No."

"What's wrong?" Sally asks.

"It's terrible." He looks at Obaachan. "The end of the world."

"What?" Sally asks.

"Watch on the TV." He runs out.

"The end of the world?" Sally turns on the TV. The expression on the newscaster's face does look like it's the end of the world. Then the picture changes to a tower and an airplane crashing into it.

"Is that the World Trade Center?" Sally asks. The picture shifts. "It is. Remember, I took a field trip there in sixth grade. A plane crash. How awful! Why would a plane be flying that low?"

Then, as the shot shifts, another plane appears, heading for the other tower. Obaachan looks at the clock. "This happened half an hour ago."

The door opens. Dad comes in. He tosses his hard hat on

the floor, then sits on the edge of the couch next to me. None of us ask him why he's home from work.

The screen splits and a reporter appears, saying the Pentagon has also been hit by a plane. Our phone rings. I hear Dad tell Mom to stay where she is. He doesn't want her on the road.

It gets worse, and over and over we watch it, the planes hitting the World Trade Center, then the buildings collapsing, like boxers brought to their knees with a single blow, the people rushing down the street, running for their lives.

Finally, Obaachan turns to Dad. "Why do such terrible things happen in the sky? Isn't that where your heaven is supposed to be?"

Earth Calls You Back

Weeks pass before I can sleep without dreaming of the towers falling, the people rushing down the street, then the firefighters running in and getting trapped. Each day there are different photos in the paper of the people who died in the attack. Their life stories are printed next to the pictures. And I wonder, if I can know some things and Obaachan can, why couldn't we know about this?

Tonight, though, I am dreaming of Matt Perino. We are walking along the river where Gregory's café is, and we stop to throw coins into the fountain.

"Lin." Mom is shaking my shoulders.

I sit up in bed. "I want to finish my dream."

"Your grandmother wants to speak to you." Mom's eyes are red. I look at the clock. It is 2 A.M.

I tug on my robe and rush after Mom to Obaachan's room. Dad is sitting on the chair next to her bed, his face in his hands. When I come in, he looks up. "Come here, Lin."

"I am sorry to wake you, Lin." Obaachan opens her eyes. "It's just that I remembered a story I was supposed to tell you a long time ago."

I feel like one of those dolls you open up and inside is a series of smaller and smaller ones. I would be the one buried deepest. "I want to hear."

"A long time ago, at the foot of Mount Fuji, there was a poor village. A drought came, and the mountain conditions were not good for growing food, so there was little to eat. In this village was an old woman who had a goose. The woman loved the goose; it was her companion. She kept the goose in the house and let it sleep next to her on her mat. She shared what little rice she had with it. She talked to the goose, and it was rumored that the goose spoke back. That summer, times got harder. Food became even scarcer. The woman was so weak from hunger, she could barely move from her mat. But she never considered using her goose for a meal. In fact, she now hid the goose inside always, afraid of someone stealing it. As conditions worsened, the village elder remembered that the woman had the goose. The villagers came to her and insisted that the goose be cooked to keep everyone from starving. The woman tried to fight them off but was restrained. The goose was taken, plucked, and placed on the flames. But it wouldn't cook. Instead, it called out for the woman. Over and over, it shouted her name. Some thought then that the goose should be taken from the flames, for it was clearly a magic creature. But the hungry, whose mouths were watering, insisted that it stay on the fire. They dragged the woman from her home and began to beat her. 'Stop!' the goose shrieked. 'Let her be. I will submit and feed you all.' They stopped beating the woman but had to restrain her from joining the goose in the flames. The goose grew silent and cooked.

"Everyone feasted on the goose, except the woman. She returned to her house to grieve.

"Miraculously, there was enough food to feed the entire village. Even more strange, each day the delicious meat from the goose was replenished, and they ate again. The villagers tried to get the woman to eat from the magic goose. But she refused. The day she died, the villagers went to take their meal from the goose; nothing was left but bones, and the bones were as barren as if they'd been lying on the ground for months. They realized then that it was love that had supplied the magic."

"How sad."

"Yes. But if you think about the story from each person's view, you will see that it is as complicated as human history."

I begin to cry. She reaches out her hand to me.

"Out of everything that is sad and difficult, something good eventually grows."

"Not always." I sob.

"Like the lotus blossom from the mud."

"You'll get better."

"What a fine thing I got to know you. Imagine if I didn't."

"I can't imagine."

"Love is very powerful. Even in times like this, it will overcome."

She closes her eyes forever.

Somehow

Two days later, Shizuko calls our house. She says that Obaachan didn't meet with her like they usually do. Then, when she was out, she thought she saw Obaachan at the flower market sipping a cup of coffee from Starbucks. Has she returned to Japan?

Mom looks startled, then gives Shizuko the sad news and hangs up. "Maybe she's nuts," she tells Dad.

In school, I have assignments due: a math sheet and a short story. Mom tells me that she will write a note to excuse me from my work and explain, but I don't want her to explain. I don't want anyone to say they are sorry or look at me sadly. So

I sit down at the vanity in our bedroom, and somehow, I do the work.

The story I write is about a world made of ice. The houses, streets, schools, even the trees are cold and transparent. Icicles drip from every building and tree, dropping like knives, shattering. The people of my story travel on skates or sleds or skis. But at night they can't sleep, because their beds are icy and their pillows hard.

Maybe I write it because I feel frozen inside, immovable as a glacier.

"Lin." Dad carries my cello case. "We have to go."

Somehow my legs walk to the car and I am taken to a service in a small Buddhist temple.

I am surprised how many people come: Mr. and Mrs. Caros, Ms. Nga and her parents, Keisha's family, the Strausses, who had occasionally talked to me and Obaachan on our walks, Mom's cooking friends, Betty, Clarabel, and Simone from Lutz Cutz, and Dad's coworkers.

Dad talks about Obaachan arriving, how nervous she was, how she wouldn't leave the house. Then slowly, she came out and enjoyed her life here. When he says that he secretly enjoyed Obaachan's Japanese cooking, a couple of Mom's friends chuckle.

Then Sally speaks to everyone in her clear bright voice, about Obaachan watching me, and teaching us to draw the Japanese characters, and I sit next to Mom, trying not to listen.

Somehow, I pick up my cello and play Fauré's Elégie, then feel sorry that everyone is crying.

Somehow food appears and people say things to me. Keisha holds my hand and answers for me. Nathan follows Sally around the room but never speaks to her.

Once we have said good-bye to our friends, we go home. Mom sets the urn on the kitchen table, where we have had our happiest times. Then Dad moves it to the living room.

Somehow, I go to my old bedroom, climb up on a chair, and take down the box that says H I R O S H I M A. I carry it to the living room and open the box. Mom says a prayer in Japanese. Then I take the ashes from the urn and add them to the ashes in the box, sprinkling them like Mom does when she's adding flour to a recipe.

As they say at church: ashes to ashes and dust to dust. What is there and then not: a city, a war, a mother's dress floating away on a river, disintegrating back to its threads, its atoms.

Melting Pot

Spring, 2007

Seeing Things

W hy are you staring at yourself in the mirror? What are you doing?" Sally is tugging on her tight jeans with butterflies embroidered on the pocket.

I am sitting at the vanity thinking about a word I learned at school: *lacuna*, which means a hole, an empty space. I'm thinking that I don't look like me anymore. "Nothing."

"I don't believe you."

"Nothing can be a subject."

"Yeah. Right." Sally looks out the window. "Why is Mr. Caros digging out there? It's like he's burying something. Do you think he finally killed his wife?"

"He's putting in a fishpond. He wants to get it in before

spring. He couldn't pay his rent again, so he's working it off."
With the money Obaachan left, my parents have bought our
house. Dad thought it would be a great thing to receive rent,
but Mr. Caros never seems to come up with the money. "Next,
he'll paint the trim around the windows."

"Ugh." Sally groans. "Dad is such a pushover, but you
know who it affects? Us. We can't have this. We can't have that.
Like, I should have my own car and not have to drive Mom's.
And you should have . . . I don't know . . . something. Mr. Caros
is shorting Dad eight hundred dollars a month. Dad should
evict them."

"That would be mean after they've been our neighbors for
so long. Besides, Mr. Caros will find a job."

"You're a pushover, too. Oh, this shirt looks abysmal. Why
are my clothes always wrinkled?"

"Because you leave them on the floor."

"Oh, yeah." Sally goes through her closet, pulls out a black,
beaded sweater, the gift from Obaachan, and tugs it over her
head. It fits her perfectly.

"I've never seen you wear that. It looks great."

"Yeah, I should've worn it, just to be nice to Grandma, but
I thought the beads were hokey."

"I picked it out."

"It's beautiful, really beautiful. I was just too dumb to know
it, then."

"Do you have a date tonight?"

"When do I not have a date?"

"Where are you going?"

"The movies."

"What are you seeing?"

She laughs. "It doesn't matter *what* we're seeing. It's a date. We're not going to be watching the movie."

"Why the movies, then?"

"You think and act like you're eight years old."

"How well do you know him?"

"What are you? My grandma?"

I look at her sharply.

"Sorry. I don't know why I said that."

I shrug but don't admit that that *is* who I see when I look in the mirror. Obaachan's face. Not mine.

"Want me to brush your hair?" Sally takes the brush off of the vanity and draws it through my hair. "Your hair's so pretty, Lin. It's your major asset."

"Asset?"

"Yeah. When I was little I wanted more than anything to look like Barbie, but finally I realized you've just got to find your assets, and accentuate them. Like yours is your hair and your cheekbones. Plus, you're tiny. A lot of guys like that. But you should get that blank look off your face. Go ahead. You haven't smiled in years."

I attempt a smile.

"See. Don't you look cute?"

"No."

"It's a fake smile, that's why. You were the most adorable baby on the planet. Everyone used to ooh and aah about you. And if it was just Dad who was with us, they'd ask if we were adopted from China. They give the girls away, there, you know. Sometimes I feel sorry for Dad that we don't look at least a little like him."

"He's happy with us."

"He's happy by nature, like you *used* to be." She sets the brush down.

"So who is your date? Did you meet him on the computer?"

"I met him last night. You won't believe this. I was working the counter, and this really good-looking guy came in with his buddies and got in my line. He ordered Chicken McNuggets, fries, and a chocolate shake. He couldn't decide which sauce he wanted, so I gave them all to him. Then he said I was cute and invited me to the movies."

"What's not to believe?"

"Do you remember Walker Briggs?"

"The fish?"

"Very funny. The boy! I didn't know it was him at first. He looked familiar. I asked him his name and he goes, *Walker Briggs!* He moved away to Texas, and only came back last year. He works at Auto Zone right down the street."

"A car mechanic?"

"A *sales*person. Don't be such a snob. He's handsome as ever."

"Is his shirt still stuck in his fly?"

"What?" She laughs. "Boy, you are off the wall. He wanted me to go out with him after work, but I was going out with Rod Parks, who is like *boring*. But this, this feels like fate."

An image comes to me of Sally walking in the night. She is crying and limping. It comes without emotion, like I am watching a movie, the mark of a true vision. "Maybe you shouldn't go in his car, since you don't know him that well."

"You were born about sixty years old. Do you know that?"

"You just told me I'm eight."

"Yes, a child and an old woman at once. The sixteen-year-old you're supposed to be is nowhere in sight. You haven't even started driving. Besides, he's not a stranger. I've known him since third grade."

"He's not going to be nice," I say, the words coming out before I have a chance to catch them.

She freezes, startled. "Don't you dare jinx me, Lin. You're always jinxing me."

"I don't." I just tell her what I see.

"You're spooky. I would like to hide you someplace. But I can't. I love you too much. And the 'rents. Embarrassing. Mother in her 1950s fashions and stupid recipes and Bake-Offs. Dad with his booming voice. Why does he have to tell everyone he's Irish all the time? He was born that way. Who cares? His ancestors were probably potato farmers. But they're there, you know. They get a grip on you that will squeeze you for the rest of your life."

"You get to eat what you want now."

"Yeah, I won that battle. And the curfew one. Here I am, forging through territories to clear a nice clean path for my little sister. What a waste. I never met such a goody-goody." She musses my hair again.

"You just brushed it."

"You're not going anywhere, so why do you care?"

I shrug.

"I hope you're wrong about tonight."

"Me, too. But just in case, don't wear those high heels."

"In case of what?"

"In case you have to walk."

Fishpond

After Sally leaves, I go outside. My parents are at a cookout in Newport, and Keisha's family is in Louisiana. Gregory offered to take me to the movies, but I said no. It would feel too weird to go without Keisha. Since Nathan started college, he doesn't spend time with us, so it's usually the three of us: Gregory, Keisha, and me.

Mr. Caros is bent over in the courtyard, laying stones into cement.

"Hello," I say.

He wipes the sweat from his forehead and looks up at me. "Look how tall you are. I remember when your cello was bigger than you."

"Where's Mrs. Caros?" I ask. Now that Mr. Caros doesn't give his wife such a hard time, she is at him constantly. It might have something to do with him losing his job. Or maybe she was just storing up a response all those years. Usually, she's out here telling him how to lay the stones, nagging him to apply for work rather than waste his time making a pond.

"She's waitressing at the Blue Road Diner."

"That's nice."

"It's beneath her."

It'll pay the rent, I think. "Maybe it's fun."

"Oh, she likes it, all right. The hubbub. Talking to people and being around food. Let *her* work for a while. Right? Let her see what it's like to wake up in the morning with a neck ache."

"Would you like a cold drink?"

"Thank you, dear. But I'm gonna call it a day." He sets down the trowel. "It'll be dark in an hour or so, although by this heat you'd hardly know it. It's coming along, eh?"

"It looks good."

"I should've been a stonemason, or a bricklayer. It's much more satisfying. Working in an office is throwing your freedom away, like flushing paper down the toilet. Like your dad, building things. He has freedom."

"He works a lot, though, and then if there're problems, he even has to work on weekends."

"True. Nothing is easy in this world. So, what are you doing when school lets out? Still playing the cello?"

"Yes. And volunteering at the hospital."

"A fine thing. A noble thing. When you were little, you were scared of your own shadow. Now look at you: working in a hospital and playing in an orchestra, attending the best school in the state. And what is your sister doing since she graduated?"

"She hasn't decided yet. When will the pond be finished?"

"Let's say, May. I like to have a deadline." He stands up, stiffly. "This pond . . . your grandmother would've liked it."

"Yes."

"She was very sensitive to nature. Not like Mrs. Caros. If Mrs. Caros sees a flower growing out of a crack in the sidewalk, she'll say, 'Why is that there?' and pluck it right out. She'll step on anything living, even ladybugs. Well, I'd better go inside and start dinner. The Missus is hungry when she gets home. I asked her to bring home dinner from the diner, but she says, 'I see what goes on in that kitchen. We're not touching that food. There are cockroaches and mice.'" He winks. "What she doesn't see is what goes on in my kitchen. But what she doesn't know won't hurt her. Right?"

"Right."

After he goes inside, I sit outside and wait for the trees to grow less and less distinguishable, then to disappear in the night. It somehow feels less lonely than our empty house.

I look at the pond. Mr. Caros's stonework is quite good. Once the pond is established, I will plant the lotus seed.

"Pssst."

I startle.

"Lin. I'm locked out." Sally's voice sounds urgent. "Are the parents still out?"

"Sally! I thought you were on a date."

"No one answered the door, so I guess they're still out. Unlatch the gate."

"I'm coming."

Sally starts to cry. "It was awful."

"Oh my God." I lead her into the house. Her jeans are ripped. The beautiful beaded sweater is filthy; many of the beads have been torn off. Her hand is scraped and bleeding. "What happened?"

"I jumped out of his car."

"Where?"

"By Providence Place. You were right. I ended up walking home, or stumbling."

"You jumped out while it was moving?"

"Yeah. I tried to do it at a stop, but as soon as I opened the door he hit the accelerator. Then I fell, and people started honking. It was a bad part of town, so I ran. You were right about the shoes, too."

"I'm sorry I was right. You're hurt."

"I think it's just a sprain. I don't want Mom and Dad to know. Get me some aspirin."

"Did Walker do something bad to you?"

"It's more what he said he was going to do. It was so creepy and threatening. Oh God. I don't want to go into it right now. He's crazy. It was terrible."

"We should call the police."

"Are they gonna arrest him for things he said? He'll just lie. These are my favorite jeans and they're wrecked. I'd better change before Mom and Dad get here. I've never been so glad to be home in my life."

I help her to the bedroom. While she changes into her pajamas, I put the kettle on—Obaachan's cure for everything: green tea. I heap lots of sugar into the pot to make it sweet for Sally.

Sally limps back in and sits carefully at the table. "Everything hurts."

"We should go to the hospital. Maybe you need an X-ray. Mr. Caros will drive us."

"It's just scrapes and bruises, I think. I hope. I feel so stupid. I've spent my whole life trying to show people how tough I am, and for what? I'm not tough. I don't even know what I am."

"I'm making you some tea."

"You're so nice, Lin." She starts to cry again. "I'm sorry I've been a bad sister."

"You haven't been a bad sister."

"Yes, I have. The whole way home, I thought about you. How mean I've been, like when I used to make fun of your cello music and wouldn't include you when I played with my friends."

"You haven't been mean to me."

"Not mean, maybe. But not as nice as I should've been. Mom and Dad were so into me before you were born. Even though I was little, I remember it. Then, when Mom was pregnant with you, she was tired and sometimes cross. It was like that scene in *Lady and the Tramp* where Lady gets pushed away by her owner. You were born prematurely, and Mom got sick and had to stay in the hospital. Dad took off work and looked after me, but I could tell, even being that young, that he was distracted. He wasn't singing or tickling me or playing imaginary games. He turned on cartoons and sat around looking worried. Then Dad had to go back to work and he hired this lady, Mrs. Crouch, to watch me."

"That bad?"

"Her name was Mrs. Crouch. What does that tell you?"

"I didn't know we were in the hospital that long?" I pour the boiling water into the pot.

"You came home after about four weeks, but they kept Mrs. Crouch until Mom felt better. Mrs. Crouch thought you were the best thing since sushi, but I was just a pest."

"I'm sorry."

"And when Grandma died you took it so hard it was like you disappeared. Your smile disappeared. And I haven't even been any nicer to you."

"Yes, you have." I pour the tea into the small cups. "Drink this. It will make you feel better."

"But Grandma wouldn't want you stuck in the past, moping. Remember how she used to go on all the time about the present."

"That's true."

"I miss her, too. She was here all that time, and I wasted it. You were smart enough to really learn from her."

I don't know what would be worse. To know someone so deeply and lose them, or not to know them when you had a chance.

"Show me how to read the tea leaves, Lin," Sally says. "I want to know how."

Café Soiree

In April, I get a job at Café Soiree. At first, my parents didn't want me to work, because once Sally started at McDonald's her grades went downhill and she barely graduated. But Gregory's dad assured Mom that I could study between customers. Besides, I only work three to six, the hours when nobody is at my house. I still can't stand coming home to empty rooms.

What I didn't count on is Gregory's habit of talking nonstop, so that I don't get an ounce of work done.

Today, he's on his favorite subject. "Why doesn't Keisha like me?"

"What do you mean? She's always doing things with you," I say.

"She likes me as a buddy."

"What's wrong with that?"

"Everything. I mean, why can't she like me as *more* than a buddy?"

"You're three years older than her."

"When we're eighty and eighty-three that is going to be a very big deal."

The bells on the door chime. A couple of college students come in. I take their order.

Gregory follows me to the espresso machine. "You're her best friend. You should know if she likes me."

What I know is she can't decide. Gregory needs a haircut. Something about his face reminds me of a cubist painting, all these different features placed oddly. Still, he's a bit good-looking. "Once, she told me that if you liked a boy, you couldn't show him, because then he would lose interest."

"So, maybe she's not showing me."

"I don't know." I deliver the drinks and take the money. Gregory glares at the customers. He hates being interrupted.

"Keisha is my soul mate. Do you know what that is? It's someone that you're fated to be with. People can meet someone and know that that person is for them, even if they're three years older, even if it's their best friend's sister."

Soul mate. If it were sole mate, that would mean there was only one. My soul mate was Obaachan. That's what it felt like. But he means a boy-girl thing.

"So here's what I want you to do," he says. "Next time we're supposed to all do something together, you pretend you're sick."

That gives me a little stab. I know that Gregory doesn't want me as a third wheel, but I thought at least he liked me. "Why don't you just ask her out?"

The bells on the door chime. Sally rushes in. "Lin, you won't believe this!"

"Hi, Sally," Gregory says.

"Something exciting just happened; something that will get me out of McDonald's."

"I thought you liked McDonald's."

"McBarf! I never want to see another golden arch in my life."

"Hi, Sally."

"Oh, hi, Gregory."

"What'll it be?" Gregory says.

"I don't have a dime," Sally says.

"On the house."

"You're sweet." Sally has this way of making boys think they are the most impressive beings on the planet. "You make the best cappuccino."

"Cappuccino it is." It's the first time he's made a drink all day.

"To go, please. I'm in a hurry." She holds up a box. "Look."

Inside is a silk scarf, painted with delicate pink and white plum blossoms and black Japanese characters.

"Wow. Where'd you buy this?"

"I didn't buy it, I painted it. It's my own design."

"It's awesome."

"I made it for my senior project and I stuck it in the closet. Then today, just before I went out shopping with Heather, I put it on. We went into REGARD, on Thayer Street. Remember that weird lady who runs it? The skinny one who wears purple all the time?"

"Yeah?"

"She loved it. When I told her I had hand-painted it, she asked me if she could order some to sell. She gave me a check for four hundred dollars for materials. I have to make fifty of them by next week. And they have shops in Boston and New York and Miami. She also has ideas about using my designs on other fabrics. She says Japanese stuff is really in."

"Wow."

"Use it or lose it."

"Here's your cappuccino, Sally."

Sally smiles. "Gregory, I swear if you got a haircut, you'd be drop-dead gorgeous."

"Did you hear that?" Gregory watches Sally leave. "I'm going to the barber right now."

The streets are crowded when I get off work, as if every class at Brown University has let out at the same time, and every business has closed. The evening is humid and heavy and my heart feels heavy, too.

"Lin!"

Matt Perino rushes toward me. "I can't believe you're alone. Every time I see you you're with your friend or Gregory."

"You know Gregory?"

"A little. From sports and stuff. That's their café."

"I work there."

"Really? I'll have to go in more often."

I blush. "What's your uniform for?"

"Hockey. I just got out of practice. It's a bloodthirsty sport, I'll tell you. I should've gone into figure skating, but my brothers would've never let me hear the end of it. So I hear you ran into Sister April at the hospital."

"Yeah. I volunteer there. She seems so different!"

"She is. Her husband used to be a priest, but now they're both living it up. Next thing you know they'll be buying Harleys and getting tattoos."

I want to ask where he saw her and why they were talking about me, but I'm still struck with shyness around Matt. "That seems a little extreme." I laugh.

"Do you like working at the hospital? It sounds pretty depressing seeing all those sick kids."

"It is and it isn't." I don't know how else to explain it. The kids will be sick whether I am there helping or not. So it's better to help. "Some of them get better."

"Do you want to work in medicine?"

"I want to be a doctor," I blurt out. I haven't actually told anyone this yet. "Maybe a plastic surgeon, but I don't want to do face-lifts and stuff like that. I want to work with people who have real problems. Have you ever heard of Doctors Without Borders? It's a group of doctors who go to third world countries and work with the poor. I want to do something like that."

"I always thought there was a lot going on in that quiet head."

"There's too much. I wish my brain was a faucet I could turn on and off."

"That would be a good invention. A switch for the brain. Can I walk with you? Everyone is passing us by."

"Sure." I search my mind for something to say. "Isn't hockey a winter sport?"

"Among fanatics, it's all-year. But my schedule. It's getting crazy, and my parents are harping about colleges already. They are so paranoid about it, because neither of my brothers went. They need at least one son to go."

"Are you going to?"

"Yeah. Definitely. I'll major in criminal justice. I think I want to be a detective like my dad. Or a lawyer. I can't decide which. I mean, the problem with being a detective is you have to be a cop first, pull people over, give them tickets, deal with the drunk and disorderly. Hockey is as violent as I like to get. Does that sound wimpy?"

"No."

"That reminds me . . ."

"What?"

"I wanted to ask you something." He touches my arm.

"Yeah."

"I could get in trouble for this. I mean, I hang out with my dad at work a lot. There's . . . you know . . . a big deal about confidentiality. The other day I was kind of reading some of his files. They're more interesting than any crime novel you could read. I never say anything to anyone about what's in them. But . . ."

Then I know why he stopped me, and my heart sinks. It isn't because he likes me or wants to be friends, it's because he wants to know about my weird talent, the reason I'm different. My voice comes out cold. "What?"

He looks abashed. "Never mind. We'd better hurry. It's going to rain."

A minute later, a light sprinkle comes. "Should we duck in somewhere? I could buy you a coffee. Or, maybe you're tired of coffee."

"I'm expected home."

"Take my jacket." He puts it around my shoulders. "Sorry if it smells."

He's so sweet that I soften. "What was your question?"

"The other day in physics, the teacher was talking about this researcher from Oxford who thinks there are force fields where thoughts exist. And they can be from other times and places. One example he gave was an experiment where they put mice in a maze and time them. Then they take other mice, unrelated to the first set of mice, and put them in an identical maze. They find that each time, the mice get through the maze faster."

"So they think the knowledge of how to get out of the maze is in a force field?"

"Pretty much. There are other things: scientists coming to the same conclusions at the same times, composers writing similar pieces of music. Then there's the day-to-day stuff. Like my mom claims she can tell if something is wrong. You'll come home and she'll say, 'Oh, you had a bad day.' Or worse, 'My baby had a bad day.' She's always right, although none of us will admit it."

I smile against my will. "My grandmother used to communicate daily with a friend in Japan just by thinking. Then, when she died, the friend called. She knew something was wrong."

"I'm sorry to hear your grandmother died."

"It was hard." I blink, glad for the rain dropping down my face. "So you were looking through your dad's files . . ."

"And I found the one about the missing boy. I just wondered . . . how you did that. I mean, there are people who work with police all the time. Psychics."

"That never happened again."

"But what was it like? I mean, how did you do it?"

The curiosity and insistence in his voice brings me back to

catechism and his questions for Sister April. "How does your dad solve crimes?"

"He gathers evidence. He analyzes it. He also says that detectives have highly developed instincts, and that they have to trust those instincts."

"Exactly." I turn and look at him. His face is so open. It makes my stomach flutter.

"Like in *Star Wars*," he says, joking. "'Trust your feelings, Luke.'"

"I've never seen that movie."

"Really? You're deprived."

"That's part of it, too. I'm not always on the phone, or hooked to the computer or the TV. You have to be still and quiet."

"Like a statue." He grins.

"Right. My grandmother said that if you were empty, the universe would fill you. This is my street."

"I'll walk you to the door."

"It's okay." I give him back his jacket. "Bye."

"Just one more question."

"What?"

"What are you doing Saturday night?"

Fishing

In June, Dad and I finally go fishing. Mom packs a huge picnic for us with deviled eggs, ham sandwiches, fruit salad, and lemon tarts. "Every bite of this has to be eaten," she instructs.

"There's like twelve sandwiches," I complain. My parents haven't noticed yet, but ever since we studied the living conditions of cattle and chickens used for meat, I have eaten as little of it as possible. I haven't staged a total rebellion, like Sally, but I'm working up to it.

"Don't insert *like* into a sentence where it doesn't belong."

"I'll take some of the picnic," Sally volunteers. "You never offer me anything."

"That's because you shun my food for McCrap."

"Mom! You said a bad word."

"I'll say a few more if you two keep it up." Mom lost yesterday's pie contest, so she's in a bad mood. "If you're going out, Sally, I'll pack you one, too."

"We're leaving in about two seconds." Sally looks at her watch.

"Who's we?" Dad asks. My parents never did find out about Walker Briggs, and the night she limped home. She pretended she had the flu for a week and stayed in bed, while I brought her meals and kept her company, just like I used to do for Obaachan.

The doorbell rings. Sally grabs her purse. "Bye!"

"Excuse me, Sally, but we would like to meet your friend," Dad says.

Sally opens the door. Nathan steps in.

"Hi, squirt," he says to me.

"Mom, Nathan. Dad, Nathan. We're going to an art show in Goddard Park. See ya!" She grabs his arm and pulls him out the door.

"Nice to meet you, finally," Nathan yells back.

"What does he mean, 'finally'?" Dad wonders.

Mom turns to Dad. "He's black!"

"No! You're kidding."

"I don't think there's anything funny about it."

"So what?" I say.

"You don't believe in interracial relationships?" Dad teases.

Mom looks from one of us to the other. "W-w-well, I don't mean anything bad about it. It's just black and white are different."

"Keisha's black," I argue.

"She's your friend, not your boyfriend. And Keisha is from a good family. Don't you two try to make out like I'm a racist. I am nothing of the kind. That was just a surprise."

"Nathan is from the same good family. He's Keisha's brother."

"Well, that's all right, then. Isn't it?"

"Is he a nice kid?" Dad asks me.

"He's weird, but he is nice."

"I just think we should keep a close eye on whom our children date," Mom says. "Here's your picnic. I would've made her one if she told me."

"Don't worry." Dad kisses Mom. "Lin and I will polish it off. Right, kiddo."

"Right."

"And we thank you, for this fine meal, all those in the past, and all those in the future."

Mom blushes again, this time with pleasure.

We drive all the way across our small state to Dad's favorite beach. Like I always do, I read the billboards along the way. There is an advertisement for the hospital where I work that shows a child with no hair. Then there's one that says, BE PATRIOTIC. IMPEACH GEORGE BUSH.

"That's a good one," Dad says. Dad's dislike of Bush is even stronger than Mom's. "It's one of those times when you want these times to pass. Except, I don't want you girls to grow up."

I smile and try not to remind him that we are grown up. Pretty much.

As soon as we hit the beach, we demolish most of the food, except the ham sandwiches. I throw those to the seagulls.

"Remember the story about the fisherman who catches a talking fish," Dad says. "The fisherman lets the fish go, and to reward him, the fish gives him a wish."

"I don't remember it."

"The fisherman asks for a nice house for his wife."

"Is the wish granted?"

"Uh-huh. But his wife isn't satisfied. She asks for a castle, then to be a queen, then a goddess. Finally, the fish takes everything away."

A koan. "She was too greedy."

"We have to be grateful for what we have. There's no other way to be." My dad's red whiskers have flecks of gray in them. It's the first time I've noticed.

While he fishes, I sit under the umbrella and work on my school report about the Peace Museum in Hiroshima, the way the exhibits present both the horrors of the war and the hope after the war. There are exhibits of destruction: a bicycle melted into an abstract sculpture, human skin in jars, photographs of maimed and disfigured people. Outside, the skeleton of a building has been left intact for the sake of memory, and there is a statue dedicated to Sadako, a girl who had leukemia, like some of the kids I work with.

Dad casts his reel again and again. It always comes back empty. Once in a while, he turns and waves hopefully. His sweetness is something so constant that we all take it for granted.

I close my eyes to rest and remember my old nightmare of running down the streets of Hiroshima. But this time, as I run past the flaming river, Obaachan is there. She pulls me close to her. Then she turns me around and shoves me gently away. "LIVE!" she says.

I open my eyes. *Please*, I pray silently, but I don't know what I'm asking for.

Still, I do feel better. There is something more than what is seen or heard. There is something that answers when you ask, even if you don't know the question.

As if he agrees, Dad staggers. His line tightens, and he tugs at the pole and winds the reel. I rush to the shore to watch him.

"Yahoo!" He pulls the fish out of the water where it flaps on his line like the tail of a happy dog. I wade into the cold water.

The fish is silver and beautiful. I can imagine it swimming, shimmering through the waves. My dad holds it up for me, his trophy.

I try my hardest to look happy.

"What?" He frowns.

"It's a pretty fish."

"It's a beauty." He unhooks it and carries it to the beach, drops it in his bucket, where it thrashes wildly.

A life for a meal, I think. "Shouldn't we put some water in the bucket . . . so it will be comfortable?"

"The point is not to make it comfortable, Lin. It's to have dinner."

"If a fish is out of the water, though, it's like it's drowning. It might be suffering." Tears come; I fight them back. I don't want to spoil my dad's fun.

"Fine." He carries the bucket into the water, and tilts it, holding the fish so it doesn't get away.

"Good catch," I say.

"Yep."

He sets the bucket down and puts more bait on the hook. I consider kicking over the bucket. I could pretend it was an accident. Dad would be disappointed, but he hardly ever gets mad.

"You want to try?" he asks.

"No," I tell him, realizing that Sally hasn't paved the freedom-of-food road for nothing. Because I will not be eating anything that has had to suffer for my sake. Tonight will be the night I tell them. I tug his sleeve.

"What?"

"There'll be fish in our pond. Won't there? Since we'll have a pond, we'll want fish in it. Keisha's mom says that they had a catfish pond where she lived in Louisiana and that people paid them to fish in it. Then, one day, two big pelicans came. At first, Mrs. King thought they were cool. But when she got to the edge of the pond, she realized that the pelicans had gobbled up her fish."

"I'm assuming you have a point, Lin?"

"It's such a beautiful fish you caught. Imagine how fast it must swim."

Dad stares at me, squinting. Then he frowns. "You want me to release it, don't you? That's what you want me to do."

I smile.

He puts his hands on his hips. "I can't believe it. I really can't. You owed me this day of fishing for like a million years and now—"

"You don't have to," I interrupt. "It's your fish."

"Yeah. Right. I don't have to do anything that you three girls insist I do." Dad takes the bucket to the water and tilts it. In an instant, the fish leaps into the waves, a flicker of silver in white foam, and disappears.

"Thanks, Dad." I hug him.

"It didn't even offer me anything in return. No new house or kingship. That's gratitude."

"You never know," I say. "Obaachan says that a good deed brings good karma."

"It better." Dad carries his gear to the umbrella and sets it down. "Now what?"

Even though I am terrified of the waves, I make Dad an offering. "Let's swim."

"Really?"

"Yeah."

"Okay." He pulls off his shirt and runs into the water. I follow him, gasping from the cold, laughing from the adventure.

"You will tell her," Dad calls to me. "Right? Tell your mom about the fish I caught?"

"The biggest fish I've ever seen!" I say.

Dreams

On July Fourth, after my birthday celebration at home, Matt and I head to the river for the fireworks.

Mom and Dad are going to a barbecue, finally getting into the habit of enjoying their freedom.

Matt and I don't talk much on the walk downtown. He's one of those people who are as comfortable being quiet as bursting into conversation.

Obaachan was like that. We could talk for hours, or sit together quietly. But then there are so many ways to communicate.

The weather is perfect. The day's hot spell brings on pleasant, balmy nights. The air feels exotic. The red highlights from the sunset are gone; there is only blue and gray, sea light, sea colors, darkening and darkening, as if the world itself is sinking into the river.

We set our lawn chairs next to a family's at the railing. A boy with a strawberry ice-cream cone sticks his tongue out at us.

"Nice," Matt jokes. "Do you want an ice cream? I could steal his. He deserves it."

"No, thank you." I laugh. "Do you?"

"Kind of. Be right back."

Matt brings back a strawberry cone. "Share this with me." We lick from either side, trying to keep the melting pink from our clothes. "I don't even like strawberry. It was just the power of suggestion."

"On his tongue?"

"Yeah." We look over at the kid, who is now facedown on the ground, playing with plastic soldiers. "Are you comfortable? Will you be able to see?"

"Yes," I say, remembering my mother's happiness when she met my dad, who "cared" about her feelings. Matt is like that, always asking what I want or how I feel.

"In all these years, we never watched the fireworks from here," I confess. "We always just watched from our yard. My family are homebodies."

"So's mine. Except for annual trips to Italy." He checks his watch. "It's almost time. July Fourth seems like the new year. For you, it really is the new year."

"How did you know that?"

"I have my ways. Nathan told me." He puts his arm around me and tugs me in close.

Sometimes I feel like I am watching a movie of my own life. It is foreign to be so active: serving coffee at the café, walking the halls of the hospital, presenting oral reports in my class, playing in the orchestra, being on a date. Then I have to pinch myself and remember not to just watch, but to *be* in it.

Matt pulls out a small box with a pink ribbon. "On that note . . ."

"Thank you. You didn't have to do that."

"I didn't? Darn."

I open the box. On a bed of cotton sleeps a small bracelet with pink beads and little shells. "It's so pretty."

"Like you." He puts it on my wrist. "I can barely see it. It's gotten so dark."

I have thought about you for years, I want to tell him, but I don't. I remember Obaachan's question, *Is he special?* He is.

There's no announcement, but a hush comes over everyone. Then a crack and a boom. A rocket of light shoots into the sky, splinters into fragments, green and red sparks radiating from the center, then showering down on the water.

A dog barks. People applaud. The ice-cream boy hides his face. Then another boom and white sparks: lotus seeds, tea leaves, hair changing color overnight. Green sparks: Irish fields, my dad's eyes. Gold sparks: my cello, Ms. Nga's violin, Obaachan's koans, my mother's brownies. Red sparks: another senseless war. Silver: my mother's hands, Matt's grin, passion-ate heart, strong voice.

The finale comes. *I am a girl with vision. It was given to me by my grandmother.* The crowd cheers. *Handed to me in a seed, a pod that felt as big as my five-year-old hand.* Matt tugs me in close as one explo-sion after another bursts open, lighting the upturned faces on the shore, raining over the water, like everyone having the same dream of night and falling stars.